Secrets of the Flame

The Power to Protect

Secrets of the Flame
The Power to Protect

Cindy Schuricht

Open, Look Within
LA MESA, CALIFORNIA

OPEN, LOOK WITHIN™
La Mesa, California 91942
www.hundredbookpileup.com

This work was previously published as *The Pig and the Dragon*. Parts have been rewritten, but it is the same basic story.

This is a work of fiction. Resemblance to any person, living, deceased, or literary, is coincidental. Plant references should not be used as a guide for what to feed your pet pig, dragon, or any other creature.

Common names have been used for plants. Unlike scientific names, these names can refer to different plants and should not be relied upon for plant identification. Some of the plants referred to as edible are easily confused with other poisonous plants or are only usable in small amounts. If you are interested in plant uses, there are many books and websites available for information.

10 9 8 7 6 5 4 3 2 1
First Edition 2014
Printed in the United States of America

ISBN 10: 0-9896580-2-3
ISBN 13: 978-0-9896580-2-7
Library of Congress Control Number: 2014950685

Cover art copyright © 2014 by Dan Miller
www.4-dan-miller.artistwebsites.com

Book design by CenterPointe Media
www.CenterPointeMedia.com

Dedicated to Matt and in memory of
Aunt Ruth and Grandad
and their naming argument.
—Fritz or Porkchop

In the last years of the great dragons, farmers moved into the lands inhabited by those winged creatures. Rude cabins and small villages appeared next to dark woods. People lived in open meadows and on hillsides with hidden caves. The dragons' habitat shrank, and they lived on the edge of fenced lands.

In one small kingdom, at such a bordering of wild forest and tamed fields, a young she-dragon laid her first egg on a mound of hay. She sniffed the egg and roared with pride. Then she scratched a layer of the cut grasses over the egg and flew to her cave.

Abandoned eggs are usually eaten by scavengers or not warmed.

However, this she-dragon unknowingly selected a mound of hay that had begun to decompose. The egg sank into its moist warm center.

Chapter 1

On impulse, the pig cradled the treasure in her jaws.

*T*he pregnant pig blinked as she peered from the crude stable. She looked for company or diversion—for anything interesting in the small open farmyard.

The cows had already gone to pasture for the day. Although not too bright, they were friendly and patient listeners. The pig looked toward the small pond a short distance from the stable. The ducks were busy diving for food.

She heard the chickens squawk and turned to see the agitated birds flap at the woman collecting eggs.

Stupid chickens! Every day the woman takes their eggs, and every day they lay their eggs in the same place. I'll never be so careless with my piglets.

The pig shook her head, then noticed the cottage door ajar.

I always wanted to see what the humans' stable looks like. Maybe I can find out why that hole lights up at night. Do they keep a little sun in there?

The pig slipped into the cottage. Along one wall, she saw a small rock cave that held glowing coals under a large hanging pot.

That's how they make the light! They keep fire in that little cave. She kept her distance and sniffed. *Mmmmm, the light smells good.*

The pig noticed the tall, narrow bucket the woman often carried outside, where she added milk from the cows and plunged a stick up and down.

The pig moved closer and sniffed the slight rancid odor now. *That smells good too.*

"Oh, no!" the farmer's wife gasped from the doorway. "What are you doing in here?"

The pig froze. She only knew the woman as the human who stole the eggs, sometimes brought food, and did other things around the cottage that made no sense. *Will she trap me in here? Or worse?*

The farmer's wife dropped her hands to her side and gazed at the pig's face.

The pig looked into the woman's eyes. *I don't think she'll hurt me.* Her fear melted and her curiosity returned. She glanced at the bucket, at the woman, and back at the bucket.

"Don't tell me a pig wants to know how to churn butter!" The woman laughed.

The pig walked to the woman's side and leaned against her leg trying to communicate. The farmer's wife reached down and scratched the pig's jowls. The pig rolled her head and groaned in pleasure.

"Ruthe!" The voice of the farmer carried into the cottage.

"Scoot! Quick! Don't let my husband see you!" The woman flapped her apron. "You don't want to risk his boot!"

The pig hurried out the door. When she was out of sight, she slowed down and made up a song as she headed for the pond.

"I'll see my very best friend.

Hope she's not crabby today.

Just can't wait to tell her

About my new friend.

Who scratched my head and smiled."

She squinted to search the muddy bank. *Maybe Duck's in the reeds again.* The pig pushed her snout through the tall stems.

"Quack!" A yellow-orange bill snapped like a trap.

The pig jumped back as quickly as her heavy belly permitted.

"Duck, it's me—Pig." She cautiously pushed her head back into the reeds.

"Well, you should know better than to come sneaking up on a mother with young," answered the irritated bird.

"With young? Really?" The pig pictured herself and Duck watching over a group of playful piglets and ducklings.

"With eggs, anyway," snapped the duck. "Close enough. Still have to care for them every minute."

"Are there many? Can I see?"

The duck stood in her nest. "There's an egg by this foot and an egg by my other foot. " The duck sat again and squirmed. "There'll be more, if I can attend to this in peace and quiet."

I'll leave her alone for now, but I wish Duck wasn't so touchy. The pig backed out of the reeds as the duck shut her eyes in concentration.

The fields haven't been plowed yet . . . hmmm . . . wild nasturtiums. The soil felt moist and spongy, and the pig's narrow hooves sank into the earth's rich cushion as she sang another song:

"Sun warming my back.

Soil good for growing.

Soil good for digging.

Not getting chased from stable or nest.

Good day for being."

She stopped to enjoy the beauty of sweet peas and yellow buttercups, but didn't eat them. She knew they were poisonous plants. Instead, she dug for the carroty roots of Queen Anne's lace but she still craved the peppery nasturtiums. *Maybe some are growing by the far fence.* She set off for the field nearest the forest.

The pig noticed a hay mound just inside the fence along the edge of the field. *Grubs! Juicy grubs!* She trotted to the pile and rooted through the moist, rotting stems. Fragrant steam rose from the decomposing hay. She pushed down and forward. Something moved and rolled.

The pig squinted to sharpen her focus. An egg, but not a chicken or a duck egg. It's color astonished her. *I see little rainbows when I turn my head! It's bigger than a chicken egg and a duck egg together. I haven't seen a large bird the whole time I've been crossing the field. Nobody is taking care of this egg!*

On impulse, the pig cradled the treasure in her jaws. The return to the farmyard seemed endless as she picked her way, alert for anything that might cause her to stumble. Her jaws began to ache and her throat grew dry.

She rested for a moment and caressed the egg with her sensitive snout. *It's getting too cool. I can't sit on it to warm it. I'll crush it. It's too big to fool the chickens into hatching it. And even though the farmer's wife was nice to me today, the humans always think they own everything . Maybe . . .*

The pig carried the egg straight to the pond and the reeds. "Duck?"

Duck's mood was much improved since she had finished laying her clutch. "I don't think it will hatch. But . . ." Duck waggled her tail, "what's one more egg? I'll warm it for you. But remember, Pig, if it does hatch and it isn't waterfowl, you will have to care for the hatchling. And I don't think that even pelican eggs are this big. Agreed?"

The pig nodded and sighed with relief as she watched Duck's pillowy body shadow and cover the eggs. *My egg is safe—hidden where it's dark and warm under Duck. And if the egg hatches waterfowl, Duck will raise it. I'm so lucky to have her for a friend.*

But if it's land fowl, will I be able to raise a bird along with my own little piglets?

Her stomach growled with hunger and distracted the pig from her doubts.

CHAPTER 2

All that was seemed not to be enough.

Everything that was, was the same. Within the egg, there had been no awareness of the darkness or the warmth, no feeling or sensation, until Everything changed with a jolt. Then a soft light glowed. The comforting warmth slowly dissipated.

And Everything that was, was different. Then darkness returned and, with the darkness, warmth. And Everything was the same as before, but known now.

Now that the sameness had changed once, it changed again and again. The creature in the egg grew aware of the darkness and the warmth. He wiggled in delight. But light also brought its own gift, for it seemed to fragment into slivers of soft pleasure, slivers that the creature would later know as color.

And there was another change. The edge of Everything grew tight and pinched; and all that was, after a time, seemed not to be enough.

Secrets of the Flame

Chapter 3

You should have a name.

The pig's pregnant belly grew and the walk to the nest by the pond took longer every day. One day she arrived short of breath and sank to her haunches. Both she and the duck gazed at the pond in silence until her breathing grew easier.

Finally she said, "I feel as though hundreds of little legs are running around my insides."

The duck complained, "You never realize just how lumpy eggs really are until you sit on them day after day."

"How are the eggs?" the pig inquired.

"Won't be too long for mine now. I can't tell about yours though. Funny thing about yours—it almost seems like an egg with a fever. Want to peek?"

"Oh, please." The pig tried to sound nonchalant as she continued their morning ritual. "I'll keep an eye on the eggs, if you'd like to go for a little swim."

The duck waddled off, and the pig inspected every detail of her egg as she walked around the nest. *Fever indeed! Its colors are glowing! Oh! I think I know what it can be!*

Finally, Duck returned from her swim.

"Do you think it's a swan egg? I've heard Ruthe say they're magical."

The duck shook her whole body "No!" as if trying to shake off the thought like the droplets of water that flew from her feathers. "It's not like any swan egg I've ever seen—lucky for us. Those stuck-up creatures are nasty-tempered."

But, as the pig returned to the stable, she held to the hope of a swan. *They look so peaceful and gentle on the water. How could they be any crabbier than Duck?*

✳✳✳

As the pig's delivery time grew closer, she stayed nearer the stable. As always, Ruthe brought food in the afternoon. Ever since the day in the cottage, the woman scratched the pig behind the ears and talked as the animal ate.

"It won't be long now until your babies are born and you'll be a busy mama," Ruthe crooned. "I hope you'll still have time to listen to me. You look as if you understand. It's so nice to have someone to talk to every day."

The pig leaned against Ruthe's leg to show the woman she felt the same way.

Ruthe continued, "I've been thinking. You should have a name. I've finally found one that suits you—Gwendolyn. Do you like it?"

Gwendolyn. The pig tumbled the name in her mind. *I like it. Ruthe gave me a name present. She is as good a friend as Duck. Gwendolyn. Duck will think it's human silliness. She'll still call me Pig. Gwendolyn. It's so pretty. Could it be that Ruthe thinks I'm pretty too?*

✳✳✳

Every day Gwendolyn's belly grew ever heavier. The days seemed longer. Her temper shortened as the afternoons warmed and the heat added to her discomfort.

In the evenings, Ruthe and the farmer came out of the cottage to sit under the stars. Gwendolyn often came to sit at Ruthe's feet and listen to the humans talk.

The farmer, a quiet man, ran his farm very matter-of-factly. But when the day's work was done, he often asked his wife to sing or tell tales and riddles. And thus Gwendolyn learned about the world of humans. The small cave in the cottage was called a fireplace, and a stick for carrying light from place to place was called a candle. When Ruthe talked about spinning, Gwendolyn understood why humans sheared the sheep. *Humans need to use the sheeps' wool to make fur since they can't grow it themselves.*

And, because a woman who can befriend a pig can imagine more than what she sees everyday, the pig also learned of things neither she nor Ruthe had ever experienced—princesses and knights, crowns and chalices, fairies, dwarves, and goblins.

Gwendolyn trembled at the tales of fire-breathing dragons and learned that only brave and well-armored knights would dare to face the large creatures.

One evening, Gwendolyn, excited about the escape of a princess from a dragon's jaws, didn't recognize her pains until well after Ruthe and the farmer had gone inside the cottage.

The pig labored past midnight when, one by one, her piglets were born. She tenderly cleaned and nosed each one. She recognized each nameless baby by its unique scent. Only later would she note their individual black and white markings.

The still-blind piglets also saw with their snouts as they searched for food. The pig's milk let down, and the piglets clamored and crowded, pushed and squirmed, until each found a nipple. Finally, at dawn, they all quieted, and the pig slept until she woke to the farmer's voice.

"Ruthe, the pig has birthed her litter. Come and see. They all look healthy."

Gwendolyn proudly showed Ruthe her children. Even the runt held its own.

Ruthe smiled. "Gwen," she exclaimed. "They're beautiful. Let's see, one, two, three, four, five, six—wait, there's another little tail—seven. Seven little piglets—that's a magical number, you know." Ruthe bent down to scratch behind Gwendolyn's ears. "I knew your litter would be special," she whispered.

Gwendolyn beamed, then turned her attention to the practicalities of motherhood. When the babies slept, she ate and slept herself. When they woke, she doted and fussed and settled arguments.

In rare peaceful moments, she remembered a time when she was called by the same names as her sisters—Daughter or Sister or Pig. Now she had a name that was hers alone. Gwendolyn felt that she somehow mattered in a way she hadn't before. She wanted her children to know each was special to her also.

How did Ruthe pick the name Gwendolyn for me? Did she make it up because it sounds so pretty? And why is she calling my babies such odd names now? I'll have to give them new names before they learn those Three, Six, and Two kinds of names. I know. I'll name them after good things like wonderful smells or pretty plants.

The largest piglet, a male, became Table Scraps. Gwendolyn knew he would get more than an even share. She named the prettiest of the litter Buttercup. The spotted runt had a tanginess to her in both scent and personality, so the pig called her Nasturtium. The others were named Truffle, Onion, Sweet Pea, and, lastly, Seven because Ruthe had said seven was magical.

Although the piglets now had new names, Gwendolyn could not communicate these to Ruthe. Every day when the woman brought scraps to the pig, she pointed to the piglets and called, "One, Two, Three, Four, Five, Six, and where is Seven? . . .There, Seven." But Ruthe never seemed to grasp which piglet really was Seven.

CHAPTER 4

The hard edge of Everything gave way!

Within the egg, Everything changed once more. A growing emptiness pushed the creature outward until he felt a hard edge squeeze him inward again. To escape the growing pressures, he tried to throw himself from side to side. Everything shook, but he was powerless to change position or to escape. He panicked and tried even harder.

The complete darkness with its warmth lifted; and, in the coolness of muted light, he rested. A low sound answered by a peeping chorus caused the edge of Everything to vibrate and called the creature back to his struggle.

Again and again, the creature used all the force his encircled panic could produce to hit against Everything's wall.

With a crack, the hard edge of Everything gave way!

What had he done? He hadn't been able to stretch the edge of Everything. Instead, he had broken it!

A painful spear of brightness pierced the fissure in Everything. The creature squeezed shut the part of himself that was hurt by this ray. But the sounds, no longer muffled, seemed harsh and too loud. He could not shut them out.

Bit-by-bit he opened the part of him hurt by the brightness. The pain eased, and the harsh sounds grew softer. The creature sighed in relief. Then he realized the sounds were moving away.

Before, he and Everything had been one. Now he was separate and alone.

He knew, no matter what, he must make a bigger opening in the edge of what wasn't Everything after all. Although he banged and thrashed, the edge held. Gradually he became aware of a grunting noise that was oddly familiar. The sound grew louder. Was it getting closer?

He pushed up again and the crevasse spread.

He blinked rapidly, seeing ill-defined black and white blotches through the crack. As his blinking slowed, the huge shape sharpened in his focus. An idea formed around a new contentment—Mother. If he joined Mother, his aloneness would end. She would give comforting warmth, even in light, and would ease the gnawing, rumbling emptiness inside him.

Chapter 5

A very odd lizard . . .

After Duck led her newly-hatched ducklings to fetch Gwendolyn, the pig left her sleeping babies to follow the bird back to the nest where the big egg shook and jerked. Gwendolyn expected to see a little beak tapping out a hole, but instead a small rounded snout enlarged a crack.

"That's not waterfowl," said Duck. "I daresay that's not bird at all." She turned away and led her ducklings toward the pond.

The fissure widened to reveal beady yellowish eyes that closed in the bright sunlight. The creature seemed to shrink back into itself.

"Your egg is already broken, little one. You can't stay there anymore." The edges of the crack spread further. Gwendolyn saw scales.

"A lizard," she sighed in disappointment. The creature's eyes opened, and it raised its head again. The remaining shell split in half and fell. A spiky tail unfolded and stretched out behind its body.

"A very odd lizard," the pig whispered. As the creature stood on shaky legs and tottered toward her, Gwendolyn automatically stepped back.

When she was a piglet, she had been warned of dragon dangers.

As chickens fear a hawk, she had been taught to beware if ever shaded by the enormous shadow of a dragon. But she had never actually seen one. She had never felt the fright of being a hunted animal. And until now, she had never felt intimidated by anything that came from an egg. She stepped back again.

"No, it can't be. It just can't . . ." Her voice trailed off.

The creature stumbled and sat. As it struggled to regain its balance, two moist wings peeled from its sides and stretched out to steady its wobble.

It is a dragon! What have I done? Terror filled Gwendolyn. She could barely move or breathe.

The dragon wobbled between her forelegs. Gwendolyn waited for it to rip and tear her paralyzed body. She jumped when the sharp tip of the dragon's tail scratched her chest. It was as if she was pricked into thinking.

If I'm killed, my piglets will die. I won't let that happen. I can lie right down and squish the life out of this dangerous creature. But she still stood frozen, waiting for the dragon to bite or show some sign of evil. *I wish I'd never seen the egg! Why do I let curiosity blind my common sense? Why couldn't it have broken on the way home? Why did Duck ever agree to hatch it?*

Gwendolyn readied herself. The dragon leaned against one of her back legs. If she dropped now, there would be no chance for it to escape. The creature made a small mewing sound like a kitten.

Gwendolyn hesitated. *Is the dragon as helpless as my piglets?*

But someday this dragon will be able to hunt! She knew that was a fact. She also knew she couldn't make herself hurt a baby. *All I need to do is just leave. The dragon will die on its own. It would be no different than if it hatched in the hay mound and no one knew it ever existed.*

Gwendolyn turned away. She tried not to run or look back. Finally, she reached the safe, dark shadows of the stable. The piglets cried for her food and warmth.

"There—what's done is done. When the babies finish eating, it will be late and the dragon will be gone."

But as she settled in with her babies, the pig saw to her horror that the dragon had followed her. Gwendolyn stood to defend her brood. The piglets squealed in complaint. The dragon approached with eyes for only the pig—eyes that widened and seemed to plead.

Gwendolyn sank back down to nurse the piglets. *When my babies are full, I'll remove this intruder. Maybe I'll even show it to the farmer. He'll take care of the problem.*

But, as her milk flowed, so did her maternal feelings. The dragon tried to push in among the piglets. It didn't snap or claw, so she allowed his approach. He found an unclaimed nipple that slowly oozed drops of her milk. He licked the milk hungrily and stared at the nipple as he waited for more.

Gwendolyn bent to sniff the reptile. He lacked the wonderful fragrance of her own babies; but, to her surprise, the dragon's faint scent pleased her. *Not what I thought a dragon would smell like at all. The piglets don't mind him. He's there in the middle and they've hardly noticed.* Gwendolyn chuckled. *Although it's hard to miss that spiky green tail among the piglets' black curly ones.*

Gwendolyn marveled at the dragon's perfectly formed tiny claws and at the luminous green scales that sparkled with highlights of the bronze, rose, and blue found in the shell. She chuckled again.

"Well, you're certainly not waterfowl. I guess Duck won't be caring for you."

※ ※ ※

"What's this?" Ruthe bent close to the litter. Mother's protect their young, but she-bears and pigs, even if otherwise friendly, are particularly fierce. Gwendolyn grunted a low warning.

"Gwendolyn, it's not your babies I want—just the strange one here."

At that moment, the pig realized she had already accepted the dragon as one of her own. She bared her teeth and her snort grew more menacing.

Ruthe stood straight. "Gwendolyn, you have something other than pig or farm animal. What is it? You don't need to care for a lizard. Come now, let me move it out."

Ruthe, Gwendolyn thought, *I love you, but all these little ones are my babies. You will not be collecting my egg as if I were a chicken!*

The pig let Ruthe scratch her head, but again showed her teeth when the human slowly moved her hand toward the scaly body.

Ruthe pulled her hand back and picked up the scrap bucket. "Be calm now. I promise I won't hurt your young." She turned to leave. "Besides, that lizard will just run off on its own anyway. No call to upset a protective mama."

The next time Ruthe brought food, she left to fetch the farmer. As they returned she spoke of "a strange-looking lizard the pig is guarding."

The dragon picked up his head from the pile of sleeping babies. He shifted his position and gazed at Gwendolyn.

The farmer exploded, "That's not a lizard! That's a dragon! We've got to kill it now! Ruthe, you help separate it from that stubborn animal you've named. Then we can drown it in the pond while it's small enough to handle."

Gwendolyn's muscles tensed as she watched to see which human would reach for her child.

"I can't," Ruthe whispered.

"By the gods, Woman! This is a dragon! One day it will terrorize these lands. Our kinfolk will curse our names if we do not rid ourselves of it now!"

"I promised I wouldn't hurt her babies."

Ruthe understands. Gwendolyn turned her whole attention to the farmer.

"You gave your word to a pig? That creature is not her baby!"

"I know it seems worse than silly, Husband, but that creature is Gwendolyn's. Look, none of the piglets are scratched. I feel that there is no evil in this dragon. If need be, there will be time to get rid of it. If the creature hurts any of our other animals, I will help you. But not now."

"We must do this now," the farmer insisted.

"We'll know its disposition before the piglets are weaned. That's time enough."

"Ruthe, we already know the nature and disposition of dragons. Let's be done with this."

"Surely it's not so dangerous that we cannot wait a week or so," Ruthe bargained. "There may be a use for this dragon. We don't want to kill it only to discover later what its use could be."

The farmer considered Ruthe's words. "We can ponder this for a short time," he conceded. "But at any sign of danger, we must kill it before it wreaks destruction on us and our kin."

Gwendolyn's taut muscles relaxed as the immediate threat to her strange baby passed. *And the farmer will help protect my piglets if the dragon becomes a danger.*

Chapter 6

The dragon opened his small jaws to nip . . .

Something inside the dragon whispered Mother would give him bits of food from her own mouth, but that wasn't so.

Other creatures who looked like Mother, but much smaller, sucked at her belly. He moved in to look and saw a drop of liquid form. He licked. It tasted good. He licked again. The milk came very slowly. He checked to see if the others also waited for drops. They placed their mouths around the nipples, and their throat muscles seemed to be moving in and out. A small stream of milk trickled from the corner of one's mouth.

The dragon tried to suck too. He bit at the nipple. Mother pulled back so quickly the dragon startled and the others complained. He tried to position his mouth more gently, but he couldn't make a seal. He could only wait for the milk to ooze, drop-by-drop. He licked hungrily and savored the taste.

The emptiness inside him remained unfilled and rumbled with displeasure. The dragon pranced in anticipation of the next drop. The other beside him shifted to nurse at the nipple the dragon was watching. The dragon shoved the intruder, who nipped at him and went back to nursing. The dragon opened his small jaws to nip back, but a squeal from Mother stopped him.

He moved to the nipple the other had left. Mother relaxed, and the dragon felt relief. He licked the single droplet that formed.

Slowly the rumbling quieted, and the hungry emptiness dulled. One by one, the others stopped nursing and fell asleep. Although exhausted, the dragon sat waiting to eat drop-by-drop.

Finally, he looked up at Mother. He felt contented and safe—even when the tall creatures came and argued above all the babies. He snuggled into the middle of the comforting warmth of the others, then laid his head on a rounded rump and fell asleep.

CHAPTER 7

Didn't I warn you?

"Pig, are you crazy?" Duck had come with her line of ducklings to see what kind of bird had hatched. "You can't keep a dragon! It will eat us all! I won't allow it!"

The alarm in the duck's harsh voice woke all the piglets and the little dragon. The piglets circled and rooted with their noses until they found nipples. The dragon watched an unclaimed nipple until a drop of milk slowly oozed out. He greedily licked it and sat back to wait for another drop to form.

Duck continued her harangue. "I have some say in this too. After all, I hatched the egg for you. If I had known it held a dragon, I wouldn't have sat on it at all. I would have rolled it right down into the pond. That's what I should have done. But no, I just rearrange my own eggs and let you put that big lump of danger right smack dab . . ."

"Duck," the pig said, "look at the rainbows in each of his tiny little scales."

The duck bent her head closer to the dragon, who looked at her and then leapt at three drops of milk as they trickled down the pig's side.

"He was one of the most beautiful eggs I've ever seen," Duck admitted. Then her tone hardened. "But looks can be deceiving, Pig. Mark my words, didn't I warn you about swans. Oh yes, beautiful as they glide along on the water holding their long graceful necks just oh-so-perfectly. But cross one and it will bite and peck until you're just a lump of mangled feathers. They do it out of pure meanness. And even a swan would be better than a dragon!

"I say lie on it, Pig." Duck's voice rose even louder and the dragon jerked his head around again. "Squash it before it gets any bigger!"

"Duck," the pig soothed, "look at that spiky tail in the middle of those skinny curly ones. Every time I see it, I just want to laugh. Look how he wags it while he's nursing. And the farmer is making sure he doesn't become a danger."

In the silence that followed, the dragon quickly rescued two drops of milk that almost rolled to the ground.

Duck watched for several moments before she muttered, "What am I worried about? That creature will starve before it's big enough to swallow a duckling. It's a shame, though, for a hatchling to suffer that way."

Starve? Suffer? The pig jerked up in surprise. All the piglets squealed, and the dragon looked around in confusion.

"What do you mean?" the pig demanded.

"I mean that dragon can't nurse," said the duck.

"All babies nurse."

"A dragon can't nurse any more than a duckling can."

"You don't nurse your babies?" the pig asked.

The duck laughed a short, sharp blast. "Lie back down and just watch," she ordered. Then she sent one of her ducklings to try. The small beak pinched the pig's flesh, and she flinched. The duckling flapped its downy wings and ran back to its mother.

"Now watch your strange one," Duck directed.

The young dragon waited for a drop of milk to slowly collect.

He licked it and sat on his haunches. The piglets pushed back to the pig's belly and kneaded her sides as they greedily slurped and swallowed. As the little dragon waited, his eyes closed and he dozed.

"Oh." The pig winced. "He's not getting very much, is he?"

"Like I said, cruel, but it'll take care of the problem." Duck turned to leave.

CHAPTER 8

Is she sending me away?

In the dragon's dream, he struggled both to escape the hard edge of Everything and to return to it. The sense of emptiness grew.

Duck's harsh quack ended his dream. He opened his eyes to the piglets shifting positions, jostling, and searching.

Why don't they just open their eyes? They bump me all the time.

Duck quacked again. A duckling came over and tried to nurse. Mother jumped. The duckling flapped away.

The dragon watched for drops until he heard Mother call out.

"Duck, wait! I don't want him to die. Please help me. What do I feed him?"

The dragon looked to Mother, then followed her gaze to the duck. *What are they talking about? Why do they look angry with each other?* He walked toward the bird and stood between the duck and the pig.

The dragon heard the duck's whisper, "He was a good egg."

Duck sighed loudly. "All right, but you're sure the farmer will protect us if he gets dangerous?"

The pig nodded, and the duck marched her line of ducklings to a grassy area.

What's happening? The dragon looked at Mother. *What am I sup-*

posed to do? The pig nodded her head toward the duck. *Is she sending me away?* He slowly walked to where the duck scrabbled at the base of a weedy plant.

"Here," she muttered through her clamped bill. She dropped a slug in front of him.

He sniffed it, then tossed it up and swallowed it whole. *More.* The dragon poked his head in the grass and looked. He found one slug and then another.

"What did I tell you, Pig?" Duck gloated. "You were starving the egg I sat on for so long. Help me move this rock."

Together they upended the rock.

"Come here," the duck called. All the peeping ducklings surrounded her looking for bugs. "No, not you—the strange one. Hurry up, reptile!"

The dragon hurried over and eyed a snail that inched toward a shady spot on the rock.

"Not yet, lizard! Later you'll be able to manage the shell. For now, eat these slugs and the earwigs too—they're small, but they aren't as hard as snails."

The dragon gulped down bugs as the duck pointed them out.

"Imagine, solids already," exclaimed the pig.

The dragon's chest expanded. Mother was proud of him. He found more earwigs. Then, full for the first time, the completely contented dragon walked over to the uneven pillow of piglets and joined their slumber.

※※※

As the days went by, Strange One, as he was now called, poked into every corner of the stable and yard. He often explored as the piglets slept.

"What are those, Mama? They look like Duck," the young dragon asked.

"Chickens. They're birds, like Duck, but they can't swim like she can," Gwendolyn answered.

"Why not?"

"Probably because they're not as smart as gnats."

Table Scraps lifted his head from the tangle of sleeping babies and yawned. The other piglets stirred.

"And another thing," Strange One went on, "did you ever see a chicken really fly?"

"What's 'see' and 'fly'?" asked Table Scraps.

Strange One tried to answer. "'See' is to . . . well, it's to see things so you know what they look like and 'flying' . . ."

Table Scraps interrupted, "I know what things smell like and taste like and sound like. But what's 'look like'?"

"It's how you see things, Table Scraps—how you know what shape and color things are, see?"

"No. I know shapes by touching but what's 'color'?"

"Color is red, yellow, and blue and . . ."

"Mama, what is Strange One talking about?"

"If you'd just open your eyes, you'd know what I mean," Strange One snapped.

"How do I open them? I don't even know what 'eyes' are," said the piglet.

"You just open them!" The dragon swatted the piglet.

Table Scraps squealed and nipped Strange One's paw.

"Strange One, stop!" Mama's voice was full of alarm. "Stop that!" She examined Table Scraps and licked him. She found no marks. "Are you all right?" she asked.

Once again she spoke to Strange One. Her voice was stern, "Never, never do that again."

Strange One shrank back. "I won't," he promised. But he didn't understand why only his anger was dangerous.

CHAPTER 9

I want to see too!

*G*wendolyn felt as though a shadow fell across her family. *Is this a warning? Will the dragon be able to keep his promise?*

All children argue and fight sometimes. Strange One misunderstood and thought Table Scraps was just being stubborn. He's not angry anymore.

Now Table Scraps pouted. "Why can he do something I can't? I want to see too!" The piglet stomped his hoof. "I'm the oldest. Why can't I?"

Buttercup wailed, "I want to see too!"

"But I'm the only one who can," Strange One boasted.

The arguing reminded Gwendolyn of her own brothers and sisters. For now, the shadow retreated.

Chapter 10

He had not seen another animal. He'd seen himself.

In a few days, the piglets' eyes opened. Strange One had answers for the questions he had already asked Gwendolyn. He pointed out that Duck, whom they knew by voice and scent, was a bird. The chickens were also birds since they had wings and feathers. But the chickens were different. Duck could swim, while the chickens couldn't or didn't want to. Strange One wasn't sure which.

"What's 'swim'?" asked Seven.

"It's sitting on top of the water and walking across it while you're still sitting," answered Strange One.

"Amazing!" chorused Nasturtium and Buttercup. "Can we see?"

"Bet I could do it," said Table Scraps.

"Come, children," Gwendolyn called. "Let's visit the pond and you can see Duck swim for yourselves."

Strange One hurried to lead the way. They found Duck paddling with her ducklings near the shore.

"See," crowed Strange One. "Swimming!"

"What's so hard about that? I can do it too!" Table Scraps walked into the water. But when he sat, his hindquarters sank to the bottom of the pond rather than float on the surface.

"I could see before you, so I'll probably be able to swim before you," Strange One said as he walked into the water a little past Table Scraps. But he too sank to the bottom when he sat.

"Hah!" Duck laughed.

In disbelief the dragon looked to Gwendolyn. "Mama, why can Duck and her babies sit on the water, but we can't?"

"I don't know. Duck, how do you do it?"

Duck came out of the water and sat beside the pig. "Just a knack we're born with, I guess."

Strange One followed the bird. "Can I see your knack? How does it help you swim?" He scrutinized the duck. "Hmm, I know! Those are your knacks." He pointed to the webbing of her feet.

"Dunce," Duck muttered.

Suddenly Onion squealed. The piglet sank into the squishy bank; the moist earth brushed her stomach. She quivered. "Mama," her voice carried both fear and delight, "what's this?"

"Mud," Gwendolyn answered with a smile.

At the reassurance in Gwendolyn's voice, Onion squatted and dipped her chin into the cool mix. "Mud is wonderful!" she cried.

The other piglets raced to investigate. Seven and Nasturtium rolled in the mud while Buttercup stood next to Onion, closed her eyes, and smiled. Sweet Pea stopped at the edge of the wet soil and sniffed tentatively. Table Scraps splashed out of the water. Onion laughed as she picked her feet up. The suction of her hooves coming out of the deep wet prints made a sucking noise.

The ducklings, curious about the strange sound, came onto the bank and tried to make the noise too. They couldn't. The ducklings and the piglets laughed every time one of the piglets made the odd noise.

Strange One watched in disbelief. *Why do they all think the muck is so wonderful? Why can't the ducklings make that noise?* He looked at their legs and feet. *Hmmm, they don't sink into the mud like the piglets do.*

The dragon approached the mud cautiously. He didn't want to sink in and get stuck. He stared at Table Scraps, who was trying to make the loudest noise possible.

"No knacks!" Strange One exclaimed. He looked at Onion. "You don't have knacks either."

Before the dragon could notice that he sank into the mud less than the piglets, but more than the ducklings, Table Scraps issued a challenge. "Hey, Strange One, I bet I can dig a deeper hole than you can. I can dig faster than you, too."

Strange One forgot about feet. He forgot his disgust with the muck. His only thought was that Table Scraps, most certainly, could not dig better than he could.

The piglet yelled, "Go!" The two animals began to dig furiously. The mud flew in all directions. Big clumps landed on the dragon's back and mud smeared his snout. His hole grew quickly in the soft, wet ground.

Table Scraps lifted his head and yelled, "Stop!"

Strange One looked at the two holes. *My hole is much farther across the top than Table Scraps' hole and my pile of mud is bigger.* He waited for the piglet to concede the race.

Instead the piglet beamed. "I won!"

"You did not! Look at how wide my hole is. It's bigger."

"Mine's deeper. The contest was for deeper. I won."

Strange One squeezed back tears of anger. He wanted to bat the piglet all the way back to the stable, or maybe give him a good hard bite on the snout. *Then Table Scraps will know who's best!*

But I promised never to hurt a piglet. He glared.

"I think you both won," Nasturtium said.

"Only one of us can win," countered Table Scraps, "and it's me. My hole is deeper."

"Table Scraps," Nasturtium reasoned, "you said the deepest and the fastest. You did win the deepest part, but Strange One dug out a lot more mud. So he's the fastest digger, and you both won."

"But, but . . ." sputtered Table Scraps.

Table Scraps has to win everything . . . or he thinks he lost. "That sounds fair to me, Nasturtium," Strange One said. He grinned at Table Scraps. "We both won."

Now Table Scraps glowered.

Best of all, Gwendolyn overheard the argument. "Good for you, Strange One. Table Scraps, stop sulking."

Strange One dipped his head so Mama wouldn't see his triumphant smile. He noticed his feet. All of the ducklings had knacks just like Duck's, but his feet looked nothing like Mama's or like any of the other piglets' hooves.

"Mama, why are my feet different from all the other feet in our family?"

"It's because . . . because . . . " Gwendolyn stammered, "because you're not . . ."

"What? I'm not what?"

"You're not . . . not the usual. Now go wash up," she added. "You don't want the mud to dry."

Strange One walked toward the pond and looked at the mud splattered on his chest. *Mud isn't so bad after all, except it covers up the pretty green—green, not black and white like the piglets!* He felt as if a small crack—one he hadn't noticed before—lengthened.

I'm just not the usual. That's all. Strange One reassured himself.

He reached the edge of the calm water. There he saw an image of a very strange creature. *How can there be room for something that big under shallow water?*

Onion came beside him to get a drink.

"Wait," Strange One ordered. Now there was another creature in the water standing beside the first one. The second animal looked like Onion. Strange One gazed so intently, he lost his balance. The knobs on his back unfolded to steady his body. Just before he rippled the surface of the water, he saw the image clearly. A lump of dread formed in his stomach. He knew he had not seen another animal. He'd seen himself.

Chapter 11

Do pigs ever have wings?"

After Gwendolyn sent Strange One to wash off, she turned to Duck.

"How do I tell him he's not of the farmyard? Do I raise him as a dragon or as a pig?"

"I don't know about raising either. The creature's not water-fowl— that's all I know," Duck replied. "But a duck's a duck; a pig's a pig; and a dragon is always a dragon." Duck's bill clamped shut.

"A dragon is always a dragon," Gwendolyn repeated. "Duck, you're absolutely right. Strange One will have to know he's a dragon. Each week the farmer threatens to get rid of him. So far Ruthe has been able to convince him to wait a little longer, but my child may..."

Gwendolyn's voice caught. She swallowed and went on. "Strange One may have to leave on a moment's notice. How do I teach him all the things that dragons need to know?"

"Not waterfowl, not my worry," Duck said.

"How will I ever teach him to fly? I can't even jump over the fence."

Duck sighed. "I suppose I can help with flying. But I'll have nothing to do with any of the horrible things that dragons do!"

Gwendolyn stiffened. "I never said a word about an evil dragon. Strange One will learn to be kind and loving, like pigs." With a glimpse at Duck's frown, she quickly added, "And ducks. But, even if I . . . we . . . even if we don't teach him to think like a dragon, he'll have to learn dragon skills. What else do dragons do besides the things we won't teach him--things like fighting?"

"I thought fighting and stealing treasure were all dragons do! Oh, there's hunting too. That's something else they do."

Gwendolyn struggled to keep her anger to herself. *Strange One is different from other dragons, and Duck knows it!*

"Dragons in Ruthe's stories tell riddles sometimes. Strange One loves questions, so I'll teach him riddling. That's not dangerous."

"Well, I've heard dragons love to guard their treasure and will do anything to get it," said Duck. "You don't have any gold or jewels to give Strange One. So how will you keep him from trying to take treasure from somebody else?"

"I'll just have to find something else for him to guard. I don't think that will be too hard."

"And what about breathing fire?"

Gwendolyn said nothing.

"Well, what will you do about fire?" Duck demanded.

"I don't know, but every dragon I've ever heard Ruthe talk about breathes fire, so I guess he has to learn."

Duck clicked her bill in disapproval.

"Fire only for emergencies," Gwendolyn added.

"Well, I can't wait to see you teach him to breathe fire," snorted Duck. "Are you going to be the first fire-breathing pig in the world?

"Pig, what are you going to teach him to eat when he needs bigger meals? If I weren't teaching him to fly, he would have to find all of his food here in the farmyard, where we live!

"How can you possibly teach him all the things he needs to know?

"And what will come of this? What if he grows into a dragon-like dragon, and won't mind you anymore? The best we can hope for is that he'll fly away."

Gwendolyn wavered. *I was so scared the day Strange One cuffed Table Scraps. But Strange One doesn't argue or fight any more than the piglets. And yet, when he grows, he'll be able to maim or kill all of us in an instant.*

"Duck, all I know for certain is that I have to do the best I can for him. He's one of my children."

At that moment, Strange One raced back from the pond and asked, "Mama, do pigs ever have wings?"

Just a short while ago, Duck and I were laughing at the children playing in the mud. I felt so peaceful. Now it feels like my world is about to crack open when all I wanted was to know what the egg held.

"No," she answered, "pigs don't have wings."

"But I'm an unusual pig, right?"

Duck rolled her eyes.

"You are not the usual, and you are not a pig," said Gwendolyn. "You're a dragon. Strange One, I'm not your real mother."

"Yes, you are!" Tears filled Strange One's eyes.

"I am your mama," Gwendolyn corrected.

"Just turn off the waterfall, lizard," Duck ordered. "She's been raising you the best she can—even though she couldn't have done it without my help."

"So it's like I have two mamas?" Strange One asked.

"Yes," Gwendolyn smiled.

"No!" Duck quacked. "Pig, get on with what you need to tell him."

Strange One looked from Duck to Gwendolyn, back to Duck and then Gwendolyn again.

"I'm your mama, but I didn't lay your egg and you will not grow up to be a pig. We must begin your dragon education since you may not be able to remain here forever."

"What? Why not?" the dragon gasped.

"Because you will grow too large and too strong. The farmer will grow more fearful of you. You must be ready to care for yourself. So first you will learn to fly."

"Dragons can fly?"

"Of course, silly, that's why you have wings. But Duck will teach you since pigs cannot."

"I'm going to fly!" The dragon raced around the two farm animals.

How can Duck ever think he would hurt another creature? She smiled. *He runs like a piglet but looks so clumsy with his heavy tail.*

"Be here tomorrow morning first thing," snapped Duck.

Gwendolyn shook her head. *How will he ever learn to fly?*

CHAPTER 12

If it's not one thing, it's another.

The next morning, Strange One rushed to the pond. Duck put him in the line of ducklings.

"Might as well get this over with all at once," Duck muttered just loudly enough to be heard.

Then she boomed, "Ducks and dragons need to be able to fly. It is the way to search for food and water. Also, flying is the best way to escape danger . . ." Her voice dropped, "such as being chased by a dragon."

Duck's voice rose again. "To fly, your wings must be strong. To be strong, your wings must exercise. Stretch them out as far as you possibly can. Now flap!"

The ducklings and Strange One raised their wings in unison, spread them out wide, and flapped with all their might. Although still small, the dragon was much larger than the ducklings. The wind from his wings blew several ducklings over.

Duck frowned. "You . . ." she pointed her beak at Strange One, "move down, way down. Don't stop flapping. That's it. Everyone, down and up, down, up."

The line of fledglings flapped and flapped, until wings, both downy and leathery, were tight and sore.

It felt like forever before Duck stopped them. "That's enough for now," she said. "Practice a few flaps whenever you think of it."

The ducklings waded into the water.

"Wait! Duck, I thought we were supposed to fly today."

Duck looked annoyed.

Strange One persisted. "I told everyone I'd be able to fly today."

"Not my problem. Your wings aren't strong enough yet."

Strange One heard giggling and a whispered "Hush!" from behind the tall reeds.

Now everyone knows Duck won't let me fly yet. The movement of the reeds showed him the pigs were leaving. *I never said they could watch.*

"We'll fly tomorrow, right?" he asked Duck.

"I'll be sure to tell you when you're ready. Just keep on . . ."

"I know. Keep on flapping."

As they practiced over the next few days, the birds and the dragon flapped longer. Muscles grew stronger.

At first, Strange One's wings lifted him just high enough to unsettle his footing and his balance. The ducklings' wings hadn't yet feathered out. They practiced without rising off the ground. Since the dragon's leathery wings were fully formed, he rose a little higher each day.

"Duck, I can see the stable!" he shouted one morning.

"Amazing." Duck rolled her eyes. "Might as well see if you're ready to fly."

Strange One bounced with anticipation and tried his best to pay close attention.

Duck gave instructions. "Flap yourself up like you usually do. Point yourself in the right direction, angle your wings back a bit, and fly. Simple."

Strange One crouched, jumped, and flapped with all his might. He rose up several feet, higher than he'd ever gone before, but he sank back to the mud on the pond's edge.

Duck watched as he repeated the attempt again and again.

"Your tail," she quacked, "try holding your tail up."

Strange One concentrated as he tried to raise his tail and flap his wings at the same time.

He continued rising and moved over the pond!

I can fly! He looked down at the still water and grinned at his mirrored image. Strange One admired the power of his wing stroke, the shine of his scales, the graceful line of his strong chest muscles.

He crossed the small pond and headed toward the trees. "Duck! Duck, how do I turn around?"

He strained, but heard no reply. Cautiously he turned his head to look back at Duck. His body followed.

"I can turn! I can turn!" Strange One whirled and snaked through the air back over the pond. *I look as good as the hawk when he's coasting on thermals.* Strange One forgot to hold his tail up and started to spiral downward.

"Duck! Help!"

"Your tail, you ninny. Put your tail up!" Duck shouted as she took to the air. "Up! Up! Up! I'll never be able to teach you to swim."

Strange One stopped flapping as he concentrated on his tail. He slowly pulled it back up to the level of his body. Although his descent slowed, his claws broke the surface of the pond. But not before he stored the image of himself descending—only later would he realize how frightening he would appear to prey.

"Flap—keep flapping!" Duck yelled.

Strange One's body hung for a moment over the water, then slowly regained altitude.

When Duck reached the dragon's side, she fumed, "Remind me never to warm a friend's egg again."

She stayed close as she made him practice more turns while holding his tail up.

I wish we'd stop. My muscles ache and I'm tired of flying in circles.

Finally, Duck seemed satisfied. "Go land on the bank, Strange One."

"Duck," the dragon gasped as he looked at the ground, which was suddenly much too close, "how do I land?"

The duck glared and groused, "If it's not one thing, it's another." She clamped her bill shut, and took a deep breath. Her voice returned to normal. "Hold your legs down and a little forward. Keep them straight. Good. Now point your claws up so the back of your foot is lower."

Strange One stole a another glance at his reflection in the pond. *Handsome. Strong.*

"When you get close," Duck continued, "stop flapping and stretch your wings out to catch the wind. It helps slow you down. Watch me first."

The duck glided to an easy landing in the shallow water, stepped onto the bank, and moved back to give Strange One enough room.

Looks simple.

Strange One circled once, flew back out over the pond, turned, and descended as he approached the bank. He put his feet down and forward with claws elevated as Duck had instructed. His wings spread out to their full width. He slowed with the resistance of the air. His feet touched earth.

The force of the wind rotated his wings. They folded back against his sides. Strange One's feet dug deep into the muddy bank, and momentum propelled his body forward. His chin led his chest through the muck. Strange One lay muddy, dazed, and a bit embarrassed.

"That's enough for one day." Duck headed toward the reeds and her own children.

Chapter 13

You need more to eat now.

"No," Gwendolyn said to Table Scraps and Onion. "We're not going to hide in the reeds again to watch Strange One's flying lesson."

Both Onion's and Table Scraps' eyes grew wide. Their mouths dropped open. *What's wrong?* Gwendolyn heard a whoosh as a huge shadow covered them all. Instinctively, she ducked.

"Mama, Scraps, everybody—look! Look at me!" Strange One glided over their heads.

Duck's taught him! How far his wings stretch! I'm so proud.

"Look at me fly!" The dragon had a huge grin on his face.

If only I could be the one to teach him everything he has to learn. He doesn't need me the way he used to.

She looked at the piglets again. Onion's mouth still hung open in astonishment, but Table Scraps looked mad.

Gwendolyn looked back up at the dragon. "Strange One, look out!" she yelled—too late. Just as the dragon turned to face forward again, he crashed into the side of the stable. Part of the framing around the doorway hung askew. Strange One fell to the ground.

"Strange One!" The cry came from Gwendolyn and most of the piglets.

Strange One raised his head slowly. "I'm alright. I'm not hurt." He stood up as if dizzy, shook himself, looked at the stable with an expression of dismay, and moaned, "Oh, no!"

The piglets laughed. Strange One looked just too silly. Even Gwendolyn had to stifle a chuckle. *Now I know why pigs don't have wings.*

Only Table Scraps stood with his grim expression. "Mama . . . Mama!" he insisted, "why does Strange One get to fly? I want wings too!"

"Ruthe!" The farmer's indignant voice boomed from the other side of the farmyard. "That fool dragon's broken part of the stable. I told you we'd rue the day he came. A farm is no place for a creature that's worse than useless."

The words "worse than useless" echoed in Gwendolyn's mind. She moved in front of Strange One and herded him over to the group of piglets while the farmer fetched his tools.

"Quick!" she urged. "Let's all get out of his sight . . . Now!"

"Why did Strange One break our stable?" asked Seven.

"Why is he the only one to get wings?" Table Scraps complained again.

Truffle whined, "When can we eat? I'm hungry."

"Just go," Gwendolyn ordered. "Faster! Head out to the un-plowed field." By the time they heard the hammering, they were too far to be seen from the stable. Gwendolyn slowed her pace and sniffed the plants they were passing.

"Here, children, see those little purple and white flowers. They're wild radish plants. You can eat them."

Truffle and Sweet Pea led the piglets in the rush to the plants.

"Strange One, I know you don't like plants, but you're getting bigger. You need more to eat than the slugs and insects that Duck showed you. You must taste different plants to see if we can find something that you like."

The piglets ate and searched for more radish plants. Strange One stood beside a jagged-leafed plant with small purple-streaked flowers and slowly took a bite. His sharp teeth impaled the leaves and stems. He could neither swallow nor spit out the mouthful.

Gwendolyn gasped. *He can't eat leaves!* She heard Table Scraps and Buttercup laugh. *Duck tried to tell me. I didn't understand. How could I have been so blind?*

Strange One tried to paw the plant off his teeth. He could hold down the leaves on his top teeth and pull his head up to remove those leaves. But he couldn't push the ones off his bottom teeth. His eyes darted as if looking for a way to solve his problem.

Nasturtium nudged the dragon. "Open your mouth." She bit down on the leaf edges and ripped them off the dragon's lower teeth.

"Thank you, Nasturtium," he said, then spat out leaf shreds. "Ugh! That tasted terrible."

"Lucky for you I like them," the piglet answered as she finished chewing. "I never paid attention before but your teeth are really pointy."

"And yours are flat on top," he responded.

"Hmmm," mused Nasturtium, "I guess that's another difference between pigs and dragons."

Gwendolyn sighed. *And it means that getting my unusual child enough food is going to be even harder than I thought*

CHAPTER 14

What's "treasure"?

Gwendolyn called out, "Now dig for wild radish roots!" The piglets raced to the spots where they had eaten the plants down to short stems. The soil flew as they dug.

Yuck! I won't like the roots either. The dragon didn't move.

"Strange One," Gwendolyn said, "you can't eat leaves, but maybe you can swallow roots the same way you toss a slug down your throat."

"But I don't like the taste, Mama."

"Since you won't chew it, maybe it won't taste too bad. Try just one."

Table Scraps lifted his head from the hole he was digging. "I can dig up a bigger root than anyone!" he bragged. The other piglets squealed as they dug faster.

No, you can't. I can find the biggest one! Doesn't mean I have to eat it. Strange One started to dig. He saw red and nosed dirt to one side. *What's that sparkle under the root hairs?* He uncovered a rock with shiny metallic flecks and gently lifted it out of the hole with his teeth.

Purple veins ran through the black rock. The sparkles brightened in the sunlight. *It's so beautiful.*

"Here's my prize-winning root!" Table Scraps boasted as he dropped a large root.

"I found one!" said Onion.

"Look what I have," said Strange One.

"It's just a rock." Table Scrapes dismissed the stone. "I win."

"Yours isn't bigger than mine." Onion laid her root alongside Table Scraps' root. Then she hung her head when she saw his was bigger.

The other piglets eyed their own roots and said nothing.

"Look," gloated Table Scraps, "mine's the biggest, and it will taste the best too. I win."

"I found something better than a root. Better wins!" asserted Strange One.

"The contest was for a radish root. You can't even eat yours."

"But my rock glitters. Your root doesn't do anything."

The two stared at each other defiantly. The other piglets watched their brothers.

Strange One fumed. *Table Scraps is just stupid. He can't admit he's wrong. He can't fly or anything. There is no way a root is better than this rock. A rock lasts forever.*

"Let's have Nasturtium decide," he said.

Table Scraps nodded.

Nasturtium moved the rock alongside the root. She looked closely at one and then the other. She sniffed the rock and then the root. She licked the rock and said, "Oh, look, it gets even prettier when it's wet."

Table Scraps frowned.

Nasturtium turned slowly to the root. Then, in an instant, she gobbled it.

"Umm, the root is best," she announced. "Table Scraps wins."

"What!" Strange One protested. Then he glanced at Table Scraps' face. *He won, but Nasturtium ate his root. He doesn't know what to say.*

"I get to keep my rock." Strange One gloated. *And I didn't have to eat a radish.*

"I, I knew mine was better." Table Scraps tried to boast, but the other piglets snickered. "I wasn't hungry anyway," he finished. He went to lie by Gwendolyn under the cooling shade of an oak tree. One by one, the piglets finished eating and joined the afternoon nap.

Strange One stayed awake with Gwendolyn. The dragon kept his rock between his front paws.

"Mama, flying is so wonderful. Are there other good parts of being a dragon? What else do I need to know?"

The pig looked at his rock. "Well, dragons guard treasure," she said.

"What's 'treasure'?" Strange One asked.

"Treasure is what you love most. Dragons sleep surrounded by . . ." Gwendolyn hesitated, "their gold, and they protect it from thieves."

"I have my rock," Strange One mused. "I like it a lot, but I don't love it, so it must not really be treasure. I love you, Sweet Pea, Nasturtium, Onion, and Seven, and Truffle and Buttercup . . . and Table Scraps too, I guess." The dragon yawned. "So I'm sleeping with my treasure. That's another good thing about being a dragon."

He drifted to sleep.

After the nap, the youngsters romped and played.

"Let's play Hog the Rock," Table Scraps shouted. He dropped a stone and crouched, daring the others to try to claim it for themselves. The piglets eyed it. Seven darted forward, then veered aside as Table Scraps defended his rock.

A sly look crossed Strange One's face. *I know how to fool him.*

Buttercup and Onion dashed for Table Scraps' stone at the same time. The dragon picked up his sparkly rock. The dust from the scuffle for Table Scraps' rock settled.

Strange One dropped his sparkly rock and announced, "I've got it!"

Table Scraps spit out his stone. "No you don't!" he yelled. "I still have it."

Sweet Pea grinned, looked around, grabbed a third rock, and shouted, "No, I've got it!" He dropped his rock near Table Scraps.

The other piglets squealed. Each one found a stone and yelled, "I've got it."

Table Scraps looked around in dismay, "But I've got the real one!"

"No, I've got the real one!" said Onion.

"No, I do!" each piglet echoed with giggles.

"You're all hogs." Gwendolyn stopped the argument. "It's time to go home."

Obediently, the children dropped their rocks and followed Gwendolyn—all except for Table Scraps. He stood his ground and shouted at their backs, "I really won!"

Strange One trotted back to his brother. "Come on, Scraps, it's just a game."

"But I really won. You cheated."

"We just got tired of you winning all the time. Nobody else ever gets to have the rock."

"But I won!"

Table Scraps always has to win everything! Let him spend the night in the field if he can't take a joke.

Then Strange One recalled Table Scraps' expression as the dragon flew overhead, right before his crash. *Scraps doesn't win everything. Hog the Rock isn't as good as flying. Who cares if he wins all the pig games?*

The dragon turned back to his brother. "You really did win," he said gently. But he arched his wings ever so slightly, conscious of Table Scraps' gaze.

CHAPTER 15

A farm is no place for an animal that doesn't pull his own weight.

When the family reached the farmyard, Gwendolyn sighed with relief. *Thank goodness. The farmer was able to repair the stable. The child didn't hurt anyone. He was just clumsy. Can't the humans see that?*

But the farmer called Strange One "worse than useless." What if Ruthe can't talk him out of getting rid of Strange One this time? I have to find out what they're thinking.

When night fell, the piglets joked and shoved as they found places to settle down. Gwendolyn eased her way to the door jamb. The dragon followed.

"Not this time, Strange One."

"Why not?"

Gwendolyn raised her eyebrows. "On the slight chance the humans forgot about your crash, we don't want to remind them."

"Oh." Strange One drooped.

"I need to find out if they're upset," the pig explained. "I'll tell you about it when I get back."

Strange One slouched back to the pile of piglets, and Gwendolyn walked toward the cottage. She feared what she might find, but she needed to know. She moved to Ruthe's side.

"I was down by the pond this morning," Ruthe said, "and I saw the most comical thing. I think one of the ducks taught the dragon to fly."

As Ruthe described the scene, a low chuckle began in the farmer's throat and worked its way down to his belly.

Gwendolyn closed her eyes and imagined she heard a human child rather than a grown man. When she looked again, the farmer wiped the corners of his eyes.

"So that's how that fool dragon crashed into the stable. Well, it was easily fixed . . . and worth a good laugh, as long as he doesn't use it as a way to land." He looked at Ruthe. Once again smiles spread across both their faces. Chuckles grew into guffaws. Flickering candlelight reflected from the tears rolling down the farmer's cheeks.

Gwendolyn's tense muscles relaxed. *It was funny.* She smiled.

"But . . ." the farmer's voice grew serious, "a farm is no place for an animal that doesn't pull his own weight."

Gwendolyn wanted to scream. *Think of something! If you humans are so smart, think of a way to use a flying dragon!*

"Maybe the dragon can be helpful to us, even if it's not here on the farm. Let's think on it longer, Husband," said Ruthe.

"Only a little longer," warned the farmer.

Only a little longer to find a way for Strange One to help the humans or to prepare him to live on his own.

Chapter 16

Aye es iss iddle oh ard?

The next morning, Duck ended Strange One's lessons.

"I've taught you everything I can," Duck said. "You fly almost as well as some ducks. Something about the way you hold your head looks funny though. Keep your neck straight."

As the piglets came to play with the ducklings, Strange One pranced off to find Gwendolyn.

"Mama, Duck said I can fly as well as ducks!" he boasted. "And she thinks I'm funny."

"I'm so proud of you!" said Gwendolyn. "Now that your flying lessons are over, there are a few things left to teach you. All the dragons in Ruthe's stories breathe fire. I don't have any idea how to teach you that. So for now, we will start your riddling lessons."

"Riddles? Oh, I love riddles!"

"I've been memorizing some from Ruthe's stories and making up some myself," Gwendolyn said. "Let's walk beyond the field while we talk, and I'm going to show you how to forage in the forest. There's a plant you might like."

Not more plants! Yuck! Strange One almost missed what she said next.

"After the rain and before the dance, I grow in a circle ever wider. What am I?"

Gwendolyn and Strange One walked through the field with their heads close so they could talk. The dragon's back was now the same height as Gwendolyn's, but his long neck and tail made him more than twice her length.

The dragon followed the pig's lead. When she trotted, he kept pace with a most undragon-like gait. When she slowed down, his tail dragged on the ground.

Strange One thought for only a moment before he said, "I don't know, Mama? What?"

"Think harder, Strange One. Figure out the pieces, then put the puzzle together."

Strange One narrowed his yellow eyes in concentration. "I grow in a circle," he repeated. "If it grows, it's something that's alive. It grows after the rain, so it must be a plant and not an animal. A circle ever wider—a tree. It's a tree!"

"You didn't figure out all the parts. It grows after the rain, but before the dance," Gwendolyn prompted. "Think about dances in Ruthe's stories."

"Hmm—princes and princesses dance . . . and fairies dance. They dance inside rings—rings of mushrooms that get bigger every time it rains! A fairy ring—that's the answer!"

"Good," said Gwendolyn. "Here's another. What grows shorter with light and is brightest at night?"

"That's easy, a shadow grows shorter with the brightest light of day . . . Oh, but it isn't brightest at night. Don't tell me. I have to figure out the other piece."

They reached the fence that separated the field and the forest. The dragon stopped.

The pig squeezed under the lowest rail. "Come on, Strange One."

"But Mama, the farm ends here. There are wild creatures on the other side of the fence. Wild creatures that could devour us!"

"Who told you that?"

"The chickens. They said it's very dangerous outside the fence. Even if it isn't dangerous, they said fences show you where to stop."

"Chickens—useless wings and useless brains," Gwendolyn fumed. "What do fences mean to robins, crows, and most other sensible birds?"

"A place to rest?" the dragon guessed.

"A place to rest," Gwendolyn agreed, "or nothing at all. They just fly right over. So never mind what fences mean to chickens. Now act like a robin and go over this fence."

Strange One still hesitated. "But what about the wild creatures?"

"You can protect me."

"Huh?" *She's supposed to take care of me!* . . . *Oh!* Strange One smiled. "I'm the biggest and I have the sharpest teeth, right?"

The dragon flew to the forest side of the fence.

Gwendolyn repeated the riddle as they entered the shadowy woods. "What grows shorter with light and is brightest at night?"

Strange One tried to pay attention to the riddle, but it was hard. The forest seemed so mysterious with its shade, shadows, shafts of sunlight, and new kinds of rustlings in the bushes.

"The moon is brighter at night." Strange One thought out loud. "But it doesn't grow shorter with light. Sometimes shadows grow or shrink depending on the light, but they aren't brightest at night. Hmm?"

Gwendolyn stopped by a rotting log. She sniffed. "They're here."

Strange One took a deep breath of the musty forest scent.

"What's here?"

"You'll find out. Just dig."

"Is it treasure?" He dug as fast as he could and peered into the hole. "Round things connected with little white roots?"

"That's a truffle, a kind of fungus. Sometimes the farmer brings me to find them. But I only show him a few." Gwendolyn giggled. "I don't want him to get them all."

She picked up a peach-sized sphere from the hole, shook off most of the soil, and dropped it in front of the dragon. "You're the first of your brothers and sisters to taste one. They're delicious. Try it."

"I'm not going to like it," Strange One stalled.

"Just taste one."

"I don't want to get it stuck on my teeth."

"Eat it the way you eat slugs."

"But slugs just slip down my throat."

"Strange One, I'm trying to get you enough to eat. Just try one!"

Strange One tossed the fungus in the air and caught it in his mouth. The gritty lump stuck in his throat. He gagged and spat it out.

"This tastes like dirt! It's horrible!" The dragon glared at Gwendolyn.

"Well, what food do you want?" asked Gwendolyn.

"I want . . . I don't know what I want. Something that tastes better than snails and is enough to fill me up."

"Well, I think truffles taste great and they're lots bigger than snails. I just don't know what to do now." Gwendolyn dropped to her haunches. "We still have to find more food for you. If you don't like truffles, I can't think of any other plant you'd eat." She sighed. "What should we do with the truffles, cover them back up?"

"Take them to the piglets?"

Gwendolyn smiled. "Good idea. You're taking care of your treasure."

"Can we do more riddles?" Strange One asked.

"You haven't answered the last one yet. What grows shorter with light and is brightest at night?"

"When there's more light during the days, nights get shorter but not brighter. This riddle doesn't make sense. Stars are brightest at night, but I can't think of any way they get shorter with light." Strange One mulled over the riddle as he struggled to stuff truffles in his cheeks.

The sky darkened as they approached the farmyard.

Strange One mumbled through the truffles, "Aye es iss iddle o ard?"

"It's hard because it's about the human world. You may need to know more of their ways, son. Think."

Strange One watched Ruthe enter the cottage. He saw a small flame light up the window.

Strange One spit out the truffles. "I know! Is it a candle?"

"Yes!"

"I figured it out! A candle!"

"And that gives me an idea," said Gwendolyn.

Strange One wasn't sure he wanted to know Gwendolyn's new idea.

Chapter 17

Mama, it hurts.

The piglets had already crowded into the stable when Gwendolyn and Strange One arrived. The young pigs grunted and pushed against each other as each tried to find enough space.

How crowded it's getting in here. Something else to worry about—how will we all fit in the stable when they're bigger? I won't think about that now. I have an idea that just might get Strange One fire.

"Come outside, everyone," she called. "Strange One brought you a surprise!"

Truffle was the last one out. Strange One walked over to her and dropped his mouthful of truffles at her feet.

"A truffle for Truffle," he proclaimed, "and one for everyone else too."

Gwendolyn grinned as each piglet grabbed and gobbled a fungus ball. *Maybe now he'll appreciate why I thought he'd like them.*

"Are there any more?" Table Scraps was the first to finish. "Where did you find them? Why did you bring them to us instead of eating them yourself?"

Strange One answered grandly, "Because you're my treasure!"

Gwendolyn raised her eyebrows.

"And I don't like them too much," he admitted.

"Now we know you're crazy," Onion joked.

"I want another one," Seven mumbled through the last of his fungus.

"You've already eaten everything that Strange One was able to carry home. Don't forget to thank him," Gwendolyn admonished. "He carried all of the truffles in his mouth."

"Thank you," the piglets chorused.

Onion and Seven started back inside.

"Wait, children, the nights are warm now and we can all barely fit into the stable. Let's sleep outside."

"Fun!" Seven turned around. "We can watch the stars while we sleep."

"Dummy," taunted Buttercup, "you can't watch anything with your eyes closed."

The piglets were so excited, Gwendolyn almost didn't notice that Strange One seemed reluctant to sleep outside. *He's the most cramped in the stable. Why doesn't he want to sleep out here? Dragons always seem to live in caves. Does that feel safer to them? Soon my dragon child won't fit into the stable at all. And when the piglets are full grown, they won't all fit in either, with or without Strange One. Where will we all sleep in winter?*

Gwendolyn's worries all seemed to clamor for her attention. *The humans still haven't figured out a way for Strange One to help them. Every farm animal contributes something. The cows give milk. The sheep grow wool. Even the chickens lay eggs. We pigs share the farm with the humans, and I am the woman's friend. Sometimes the farmer takes me to hunt truffles, and the piglets will learn that too.*

There has to be some way a flying dragon can help the humans. But what?

Nasturtium was the first piglet to settle on a spot. Seven laid his head across her back. Buttercup used Nasturtium's neck for a pillow.

Table Scraps plopped down partially atop Seven, who squirmed to get comfortable again. One-by-one, the piglets came to the pile.

Gwendolyn motioned to Strange One to follow her to the cottage.

If Ruthe tells stories by candlelight tonight, we can try my idea. If it doesn't work, I just don't know. Is Strange One ready? I don't even know ready for what? How long does he have?

Gwendolyn and Strange One curled on the dirt by the log where Ruthe sat. Gwendolyn paid no attention to the human's words. She stared at the candle stuck to a rock with wax. The candle burned low.

Ruthe stood. "I'll get tea. Will you get another candle?" she asked the farmer. The humans went into the cottage.

"Strange One," Gwendolyn whispered, "start back towards the stable."

"I want to hear the end of the story."

"Not tonight. Hurry!"

He ambled away.

Gwendolyn bit the base of the burning candle stub and moved as quickly as she could, while shielding the flame with her body. The flame flickered and sputtered, but didn't go out.

"Strange One," she hissed, "turn around." The golden yellow of his cat-like eyes led her to him. Gwendolyn carefully set the stub upright in front of him.

"Eat this."

Strange One eyed the candle. "I already had to try a truffle today, Mama. Why do I have to eat a candle?"

"This isn't food. I hope the flame will light your dragon fire. Eat it before the flame goes out. "

"Eat it while it's lit? This was your new idea? I'll get burned!"

"Do dragons get burned when they breathe fire? No. Eat the candle now."

Strange One bent over the candle and stopped.

"Eat it in one gulp, Strange One. I mean it."

Strange One tensed his muscles and wolfed down the candle. He yelped in pain and ran toward the pond. Gwendolyn ran after him.

"Strange One, don't take a drink! Try to blow fire."

The dragon opened his mouth and huffed. "Mama, it hurts."

"Let me look."

Strange One's throat was as dark as the night—no glow, no flame, no spark. "I'm so sorry, Strange One, but we had to try something. You may as well get a drink. Now I don't know what to do or who to ask."

Gwendolyn's stomach tightened with dread as she realized she did know who she would have to ask. *Dragons themselves are the only ones who can tell me how they get fire.*

CHAPTER 18

The monster ate my babies!

Strange One sat back on his haunches. *Yesterday I gave the piglets the best thing a pig can eat, and Mama gave me a burning candle! The only thing I can swallow now is a slug. Even with slime it hurts my throat.*

"It's not fair!" he said aloud to no one in particular. *I just want to eat enough food that I like. Is that too much to ask? What's worse, Mama's getting ready to find some dragons. But is she taking me along? No! Even though I'm the one who needs fire. I'm the dragon—not her!*

He searched for Gwendolyn and argued, "You said yourself, I might have to deal with dragons if I leave the farm. Now would be the perfect time to learn."

"You can't come along, Strange One. You're too big and too squirmy to hide and stay still."

"I could stay still if my throat didn't hurt so much."

"I'm sorry. The candle was a bad idea. Let me see your throat."

Strange One snapped his jaws shut and shook his head.

"Strange One, open your mouth," Gwendolyn insisted.

She can't make me. The dragon knew he now had the power. *She isn't even my real mother, she said so herself. A real mother wouldn't make me eat a burning candle.*

Strange One walked over to the chickens. *I'll show her. Today I'll learn something from the chickens.*

He couldn't think of anything to ask them, so he sat with his back to Gwendolyn. *I'll just act like they're telling me something really interesting.* He noticed an abandoned egg partially hidden in the far grass.

Strange One remembered seeing a broken egg once. *A golden ball in thick water. Just thinking about swallowing it feels good on my throat. The humans eat eggs.*

I wonder what they taste like. The shells would probably hurt my burned throat. Strange One noticed a second egg in the weeds. *Nobody's sitting on them. They're not going to hatch anyway.*

But still he hesitated, until the chickens turned their attention to Duck, who landed near the stable.

Strange One knew that Gwendolyn had asked Duck to fly over the forest to look for signs of dragons. He looked away but strained to hear Duck's words.

"I met a bluejay. He knows about a she-dragon with a brood that will soon leave the nest. The jay said the dragon lives in a high cave that faces the setting sun. Come to the road and I'll show you. I still think you're daft, Pig." Duck shook her head. "Dragons!"

The chickens edged closer to the duck. Strange One knew they hoped to hear a bird put the pig in her place. He stayed put.

I'm not going to say anything to her. She may have to sit for a long, long time before she hears a dragon talk about fire. I bet she can't sit still that long either.

Strange One tried to ignore his growing fear that something could happen to Gwendolyn or that she might not be back by the time it got dark. How would he be able to sleep?

He looked out of the corner of his eye as the piglets encircled Gwendolyn to tell her goodbye. Buttercup begged her to stay. When Strange One saw Gwendolyn look over the backs of the piglets, trying to catch his eye, he stared at the ground. *I'm not going to whine like Buttercup.*

He looked up and saw Gwendolyn trot off behind the low-flying duck.

She didn't even come over to make me say goodbye! Strange One flared. He whipped his head around and snapped up an egg. The bits of shell poked at the roof of his mouth and scratched his sore throat. But he didn't care. It made him forget that he wanted to cry.

That tastes wonderful! And nobody saw me. He snapped up the second egg.

"My babies," a chicken wailed. "The monster ate my babies!"

The rooster charged along with the distraught chicken. Other hens quickly gathered their chicks under their wings and eyed the dragon with reproach and fright.

"But they weren't babies. She wasn't sitting on them anyway," Strange One protested. He turned his head away from the flapping wings and fierce beak of the enraged rooster. Although now much larger than the rooster, the bird had pecked and intimidated the dragon when he was a baby. Strange One acted as he had when smaller. He huddled to keep his eyes safe from the sharp claws.

"Why won't you listen to reason?" the dragon asked the angry bird.

When the rooster finally began to tire, he screeched, "You murderer! You cannibal! Your mother will hear of this when she returns. Now get away from us."

Strange One moved slowly to join the piglets who stood watching the speck that was Gwendolyn. They ignored the hysteria of the chickens, who suffered crises daily.

Buttercup whimpered, "I hope Mama gets back soon."

"So do I," added Onion.

Table Scraps crowed, "Now we can do what we want. Nobody can tell us when to go to sleep or anything. Right, Strange One?"

"Oh, right," agreed Strange One. *The chickens can't tell on me because Mama's not here.* He should have felt happy, but a part of him thought there was no one to help him set things right.

By late afternoon, the chickens seemed to have completely forgotten the eggs. Strange One had not.

CHAPTER 19

I might never find my way back!

Duck landed on the road near Gwendolyn, "Pig, this journey is too dangerous for a farm animal. Why risk your life for something you may never find anyway?"

"Don't you risk your life to lure a hawk away from your babies?"

"I do when my babies are little, but not when they're bigger than me! And why are you trying to find a way to make Strange One more dangerous?"

"Unless the humans think of a way to use a flying dragon, the farmer won't let him stay much longer. Maybe Strange One will need fire to protect himself."

"Protect himself from what?" sputtered Duck. "He's already bigger than any of the other farm animals. He can fly away from wolves or bears. What else does he need protection from?"

"Maybe other dragons?"

"Maybe," snorted Duck. "And maybe if you find the she-dragon, maybe she will eat you. Or, if she maybe doesn't eat you and you hide until the snows come, maybe she'll never happen to mention how dragons get fire."

"You said yourself the young ones are about to leave the nest," said Gwendolyn. "If their mother has to teach them, now would be the time, wouldn't it?"

"You are the stubbornest animal I've ever known! Well, if you find out, let me know. My ducklings need more protection than Strange One does. Maybe they can learn to breathe fire too!"

Duck pointed her beak to a distant mountain. "That's the mountain the jay told me about. Too bad you can't fly straight there like a bird can, eh?" she needled. Her voice softened. "Be safe, Pig, and don't take too long. Your young ones will be worried."

"I'll be careful, and I'll be back soon," Gwendolyn promised.

Duck flew back to the farm, and Gwendolyn walked away from home. But without Duck trying to argue her out of going, Gwendolyn's own doubts grew, and she argued with herself. The forest edging the road thickened.

"I'm not a forest animal," she said aloud. She moved to the center of the road between wagon wheel ruts as far as she could get from the trees, bushes, and shadows—shadows that could hide wild creatures.

I'm not a traveling animal. I want to go home. But her hooves kept moving toward the mountain. A rustle in the bushes made her jump.

"I'm not a fighting animal," she whimpered. She remembered Ruthe reaching to pick up Strange One. Gwendolyn made the same threatening grunt she had then. The rustling in the bushes stopped. She grunted again—louder this time. She felt braver.

"I'll risk anything for my children . . . anything," she said. She growled. "I've been scared every day since the farmer threatened to kill Strange One. If I risk this journey and learn what Strange One needs to know, maybe I won't be frightened or worried anymore. If I go back to the farm now, I'll never know."

Gwendolyn noticed the bright sunshine, the blue sky, the still-cool air of the morning. She hummed,

"Sun warming my back.

Road good for walking.
Day good for learning
About caring for children
And having adventure."

The sun grew hotter, but she found no water—not even a small puddle in one of the ruts. It was afternoon before the road ran aside a small brook. Gwendolyn drank deeply, then lay to rest in the shade. Her muscles ached in a way she had never known before. She yawned. Even her jaws were sore. She checked the angle of the sun.

"Can't stop yet. Too much light left in the day." Wearily she stood, drank again, and walked to the road. Within a short distance, the road curved going away from the mountain.

Gwendolyn faltered. A farm pig doesn't travel, but at least traveling on a road was part of her world—a world that was already bigger than yesterday's world. *If I turn around, the road will take me home. But if I leave the road and go into the forest, I might never find my way back!*

"I'm not a forest animal," she repeated. The pig thought fondly of the other farm animals—ducks, sheep, cows, chickens . . . chickens! "The chickens tried to teach Strange One to be afraid. A chicken would never even think about going on a quest. I am not a chicken."

Gwendolyn set her jaw and looked up at the mountain. The peak looked rocky and barren in the late afternoon sun. A half-hidden ribbon of sparkling silver peeked through the trees that covered the lower part of the slope.

"The stream!" she said. "It flows down from the mountain. I can follow it up and back down later to find the road again! A farm pig on a quest may be rare, but it is not impossible." She growled and felt brave again.

Traveling through the thick of the forest took longer than going by road, but it was cooler. Sometimes she walked through the shallow waters of the stream to sooth the aching of her feet.

Occasionally, she ambled through a clearing, where she welcomed the rays of the setting sun. Before Gwendolyn had time to forage or to seek a safe place to sleep, the sun suddenly dipped out of sight.

As darkness snuffed out the day's light, the pig nested in fallen leaves under a roof of branches. She heard a screeching overhead, and inched back until her haunches touched the comfort of the tree trunk. When she looked through the criss-crossed branches, she held her breath at the sight of a she-dragon leading a flock of young dragons through the dusky sky.

The goal is nearer than I thought. She shuddered.

For hours, Gwendolyn startled at every sound or movement in the bushes. Finally, the soothing sound of the slow-moving water lulled her. She dozed.

She dreamed of climbing a mountain—going higher and higher, as she drew closer to the sound of a roaring waterfall. She woke with a start and a realization—the sound of the waterfall was really a growl.

Two yellow eyes stared at her from a curtain of black. Still groggy, she wondered what Strange One was doing. A twig crackled, and the eyes moved closer. Gwendolyn's mind cleared as moonlight illuminated a set of enormous fangs.

Wolf!

Gwendolyn panicked and bolted. She ran not knowing where she was going. She barely missed trees and boulders. As her wits returned, she knew she would not be able to outrun a wolf for long.

Where can I hide? She felt the wolf's hot breath on her rump. Terrified, Gwendolyn pulled her back legs up to her front ones as she raced for her life. Suddenly, there was no ground beneath her hooves. She flailed in a futile effort to find footing.

I'm falling! At that instant she landed in a deep patch of prickly canes. The fragrance of bruised mint leaves filled her nostrils.

In the moonlight, Gwendolyn saw the silhouette of the wolf as he paced back and forth along the edge of the cliff. He sniffed at the spot that held the last traces of her scent.

She trembled. She wouldn't have jumped if she had seen the height of the cliff. But the fall saved her from the wolf. The prickly canes and the mint cushioned her fall. The prickers scratched and poked her on all sides, but she dared not move or make a noise.

I hope the mint smell is strong enough to throw him off my trail.

The wolf turned and disappeared from her view, but Gwendolyn didn't know if he was gone or finding a path down the cliff.

I'm safest here. I'll have a horrible time getting out in the morning with all these stickers, but . . . she smiled, *if the wolf comes, he'll have an even worse time with his long fur. He'd get so tangled up, he might never get out.*

She settled in as best she could and rested.

Dawn found Gwendolyn tired, achey, and happy to be alive. She nuzzled her scratches and bruises, checked for more serious injuries, and found none. She stood on wobbly legs and surveyed her tangled cage of prickly canes.

Raspberries! I'm so lucky! She ate all the ones within reach.

She forged ahead and ignored all the prickers except for the ones that grabbed her tender ears or snout. For those she slowed to gently wiggle free.

Once she escaped the canes, she closed her eyes and cocked her head to one side. She heard the gentle flow of wind or water, but felt no breeze. "Well, of course, mint wouldn't be far from water."

Gwendolyn found the stream again and sat. The water cooled the warmth of her bruises and the burning of the scratches. She drank deeply and thought about how long it seemed since she'd been home with her children.

"I can't wait until I'm there again, but first . . ." she focused on the scorched, barren peak, "I have a mountain to climb."

Chapter 20

Strange One's a hero.

Strange One searched the road as far as he could see. *Why is Mama taking so long? Why did she leave before I had a chance to talk to her?* Guilt and shame hung heavy on the young dragon. *The chickens don't even remember the eggs. Duck and the piglets don't know. Am I really a murderer?* Strange One shook his head trying to throw off the tormenting thoughts.

"Come on, Strange One, let's go to the field," urged Table Scraps. "Let's do something! Are you sick? What's wrong?"

"Nothing," the dragon answered, although he indeed felt sick. *Table Scraps will just laugh if I tell him my chest aches. If I tell him why, he'll probably tease me about being a cannibal. Or maybe he'll be scared of me and not say anything. That would be the worst of all.* "Nothing." he said again.

Table Scraps gave up and asked Onion to play.

The humans approached. "I don't know why she left," the woman said. "But I just don't think the dragon ate her. We haven't found blood or hooves or anything. And the dragon hasn't eaten as much as a chicken. If one of the piglets had vanished out of thin air, I might worry, but a full-grown sow? It makes no sense."

The farmer glared at Strange One and demanded, "Well, where is she if he didn't eat her?"

Strange One heard the suspicion in the farmer's voice. He thought the farmer must know about the eggs and that was why the man now thought the dragon a murderer.

Strange One railed against the injustice. *The humans take eggs all the time, and he thinks I'm the murderer! He thinks I ate my own mother! I wish I'd never seen those eggs. I wish those stupid chickens would take care of them if they're so precious.*

The farmer's shoulders slumped. "You're right," he acknowledged. "There are no signs she was eaten, and the piglets certainly aren't afraid of the dragon."

Strange One went into the stable and lay with his back to the entryway. He refused to budge when Seven rushed in.

"Come outside and see. The farmer is building a fence to keep us in so we can't run away like our 'fool mother.' Won't he be surprised when she comes home, and he finds out he built a fence for no good reason?" Seven stamped the ground and laughed heartily.

Strange One stayed in his corner. Now he remembered the farmer had agreed with Ruthe that the dragon didn't eat the pig. But Strange One knew he had eaten the eggs. What else would tempt him? When would Mama get back? And would he have the courage to admit to her what he'd done?

That night, Strange One slept fitfully.

He heard rustling from the chicken coop before the hens themselves did. The dragon cocked his ears trying to make sense of the sounds. At the instant he heard a muffled "Help!" Strange One started for the coop.

A red fox emerged with a struggling hen clamped in its mouth. The fox moved aside as if to indicate, "Plenty for all."

When the fox turned to head back to the woods, Strange One caught the predator firmly in his teeth and shook. The fox released the hen with a scream of surprised pain.

The hen flapped to the ground. The rooster rushed to her side and crowed with all his might.

Again and again, Strange One shook the fox until its body hung limp and lifeless. When the dragon heard a shout from the cottage, he dropped the body to the ground. Only then did he notice that the animal, who looked so large and fierce when it carried the chicken, was actually small.

Strange One stared at the body for a moment more, then asked the hen, "Are you hurt?"

"A bit, but thanks to you, it's nothing serious." The hen looked at Strange One with admiration.

The rooster added, "We'll all sleep better knowing that fox won't come around again."

The piglets watched wide-eyed from the stable.

"Strange One's a hero," said Buttercup.

The dragon felt as if he were moving in a dream. He'd acted without thinking. By the time the farmer and Ruthe reached the coop area, the chickens started to calm down.

The farmer walked over to the dead body of the fox and poked it with his toe. "Saved my chicken, did you, dragon? Really, you saved my flock. That fox would come back every night until not one bird was left. Tomorrow I'll skin this poacher and you, my fine dragon, can eat the meat. You earned it."

Strange One squirmed. Something felt wrong. Now that the danger to the farm animals passed, the dragon realized the fox was hungry. Maybe it was a mother with kits to feed.

When he ate the eggs, which weren't even chickens, he'd been called a murderer. Now he was a hero, but he didn't feel good about it.

Why didn't I just chase the fox away after it dropped the chicken? How can I put things right? Where is Mama?

CHAPTER 21

Where can I hide—fast?

Gwendolyn followed the stream and stopped to look up. She caught a glimpse of dragons flying silently overhead as they returned to their mountaintop. She whispered thanks for the covering of the trees.

It looks like the dragons sleep during the day so I should be safe when I climb past the tree line. . . but . . . Fear knotted her stomach. Gwendolyn's legs shook, and she dropped to her knees.

I've seen dragons twice now without them seeing me. I won't always be so lucky. Maybe I should go home now.

What am I thinking? Explain to Duck that I quit? I've gotten this far. I'm too close to go home now.

Gwendolyn marshaled all her determination and leaned into the steep climb.

When the trees began to thin, she got her last drink from the tiny run of water. She rolled in mint, crushing as much fragrance out of the leaves as she could.

The mint helped to confuse the wolf. Maybe it will help with dragons too. Won't hurt to try.

She plucked as many stems of the herb as she could carry. She knew holding a mouthful of mint stems all day would make her thirstier, but, if the scent on her skin faded, she would still have some extra leaves.

When she passed the very last of the trees, she kicked several rocks together to show herself where to reenter the forest. Then she left camouflage and shade behind as she stepped onto soil blackened by the scorching flames of dragon breath.

The hot sun beat down, yet fear sent cold shivers down Gwendolyn's spine. She hurried to reach the dragon cave and hide before the dragons flew that night. One hundred times she thought of her piglets and started to turn back down the mountain. One hundred and one times she thought of Strange One and kept climbing.

Whenever she changed direction, Gwendolyn kicked a pile of rocks to mark her route. Planning for her return calmed her.

Late in the afternoon, the sun shone in her eyes. She squinted at the peak. *Finally I'm truly close to the top. I have to find their den before sunset . . . the right cave and a good hiding place.* She swallowed.

Finding the cave was easier than she first thought. There was only one cave opening that faced the sunset and had an opening large enough for the she-dragon to go in and out.

Now where can I hide—fast? It's almost time for the dragons to fly! Gwendolyn ducked behind a small boulder near the cave, but knew she would be spotted as soon as the dragons flew overhead. She peered around all sides of the boulder. *I can't risk making too much noise walking around searching. It's so barren up here! What will I do if this is the best place I can find?*

At first, her vision passed over a large shadow on a huge rock face that framed the cave entrance. Then Gwendolyn realized there was nothing to cast a shadow.

It's really hard-to-see. Looks like a crack I can just fit into. And those gray boulders will block me from the dragons' view. I hope.

Gwendolyn could make out sounds of movement coming from

the cave. She hoped that the dragons would be loud enough to mask the sounds of her own dash to the crack. There wasn't room to turn around so she backed into the tight space until even the tip of her snout was in shadow. She could just glimpse a small section of the ledge outside the cave entrance.

The sun disappeared. Gwendolyn held her breath as young dragons emerged from the cave. They blinked in the dim light, then stretched and yawned, shoved and jostled to find space on the ledge overhanging the valley below. A large she-dragon was the last to leave the cave.

"Clumsy!" she snapped at one youngster who was slow to get out of her way.

Another young dragon asked, "Where will we hunt tonight, Mother?"

The she-dragon ignored him, surveyed her brood, and spoke in a low growl that Gwendolyn strained to understand.

"Tonight is special. I will show you a patch of weeds that humans call bachelor's button."

"Why is tonight special?" a third young dragon asked.

"If you hold your tongue, you will see," rebuked the mother.

The first dragon asked, "Why are we going to see a patch of weeds when we should go hunt . . ."

Before his question was even finished, another young dragon asked, "Why do the humans call the weed bachelor's button? What's the real name?"

With mounting irritation in her voice, the she-dragon responded, "If you were a dragon who valued her riddling, you would wait to figure it out for yourself. Tell me when you think you know. And do not hang your head like a pup or we shall forget you are a dragon and devour you."

The dragon who had been ignored persisted and asked again, "When will we hunt tonight, Mother?"

This time the she-dragon turned to eye him icily. "We won't," she growled. "Fly!"

One at a time, the dragons leapt off the ledge with wings outstretched. Gwendolyn watched in awe. The moonlight glimmered and illuminated the wings that were spread taut and smooth.

"What beautiful and repelling creatures they are," Gwendolyn whispered through teeth that still clamped the wilting mint. "And what's so special about bachelor's buttons besides the terrible smell?"

When she was sure they had all flown off, the pig walked out onto the ledge. The mint drooped from the corners of her mouth. She dropped the stems to the ground, spread them with her hoof, then lay down and rolled on her back. She squealed; she had never been so sunburned. But the leaves still released some scent so she continued.

She stood, and the coolness of the night chilled her burned skin. She shivered as she turned to enter the cave, then stopped to return and kick the mint stems over the side of the ledge so there would be no sign that a stranger had come.

The moon provided a soft glow as the pig entered the forbidding cave, which soon widened into a large chamber. In the dimly reflected light, Gwendolyn saw goblets, coins, and jewels that littered the floor in nest-like piles. A number of smaller tunnels and crevices lined the large central chamber. She squinted into the openings. Most had several treasures lying together near a wall.

Are these sleeping chambers for the young dragons? she wondered. *Do they learn to guard their treasure from their brothers and sisters?*

Gwendolyn found a narrow crevice for a hiding place. It was just big enough for her, but too small for even the runt of the dragons. It was deep enough that she would be able to get beyond the reach of their claws if discovered. She settled in for the vigil and for another lonely night away from home.

CHAPTER 22

Maybe tomorrow everything will be back to normal.

At dawn's first light, the rooster crowed about the triumph over the fox. Incredibly, the chickens remembered that Strange One had saved one of their flock. In the light of day, Strange One's anguish melted.

Duck came rushing to the stable as soon as she heard.

"Well, well, well," she beamed. "I guess I figured you wrong. Not only are the piglets your treasure, the whole barnyard is!"

"Killed that fox with one shake, I heard. Good for you, Strange One."

The dragon grinned.

Ruthe came out of the cottage with some brightly colored cords and fussed over the dragon. She planned to make some kind of decoration for him to wear.

Strange One puffed out his chest.

"If I'd heard the noise first," said Table Scraps, "I could have chased that fox off and saved the chickens!"

Strange One didn't have to say a word.

"Oh, Table Scraps," sighed Nasturtium. "You couldn't have killed it like Strange One did. It would have just come back another night."

"Not after I finished scaring it," asserted Table Scraps. "Besides, I could kill a fox . . . maybe."

Buttercup and Seven twittered. "You heard what the farmer said, with Strange One, we're even safe from wolves."

Table Scraps sulked, and Strange One swaggered across the farmyard.

When the farmer came with the skinned body of the fox, Strange One gulped the meat without a qualm. He had never eaten so much food at one time. *Slugs, snails, or eggs are good, but they're so little, I can never get full. But now . . .*

The dragon burped, then watched in contentment as the farmer returned to work on the nearly completed fence.

Table Scraps came and sat beside Strange One. "It's just stupid for him to build that. You can fly over it and I can dig under anything. That fence can only keep us in when we want to be kept in, right? And we'll protect everybody inside!"

The farmer looked up, almost as if he had understood the piglet and said, "This fence won't enclose you for long, dragon. Someday you'll have castle grounds for your yard and you'll protect our king instead of chickens."

Strange One felt as though he would burst with pride.

Table Scraps mumbled, "Why do you get everything?"

"I don't," the dragon answered. "You always win Hog the Rock and digging contests." *But some contests are better.* He smiled sweetly at Table Scraps, who stomped away again.

All day Strange One patrolled the perimeter of the fence. The chickens clucked happily, never for a moment forgetting the dragon's bravery. Each one told the others exactly where she was when the fox broke into the coop and how close the predator's jaws were. The hen, who was actually snatched, hobbled around the yard with one wing drooping dramatically. But she was long forgotten as the others cackled on about their own rescue from the jaws of death, thanks to—who could have imagined—a dragon.

Strange One had never felt so strong, so wise, so valuable. But, by and by, all the stories sounded monotonous, even to him. And he wished Table Scraps would stop sulking.

Finally, the sun set. The chickens went into the coop to their roosts. The pigs and Strange One entered the stable. Table Scraps still didn't speak, but he pushed in next to Strange One as the brood settled in for the night.

The tangle of the litter's babyhood sleep had grown into a hill-side of soft snorts and snuffles. Occasionally there was a short, half-awake argument as one pig slept too heavily on another. But always, after readjustment, the animals fell back asleep with the comforting touch of the others' bodies.

Strange One closed his eyes with relief. *Finally, no chicken chatter. I never knew quiet could be such a beautiful sound. And I'm glad Table Scraps came to sleep next to me. Maybe tomorrow Mama will come back and everything will be back to normal.*

But, in the quiet of the night, the dragon's fears and guilts returned to prick and question his conscience. Again, Strange One imagined the fox trying to take food back to hungry kits, just like Mama was trying to bring fire back for him. Maybe a dragon would shake the life out of Mama as easily as Strange One had snapped the life from the fox.

Maybe he and the piglets would wait forever, just like the fox's babies, who would never see their mother again.

Those poor babies, Strange One mourned, *waiting and waiting and never knowing what happened to their mother.* But the pain he felt for the kits was really the agony he imagined if Gwendolyn never came home—agony and guilt. *If Mama doesn't come back, it will be my fault. She wouldn't have left if she wasn't trying to find out the secret of fire. And now I don't need it. The farmer's happy with me. What's taking Mama so long?*

And one other specter haunted him from the farthest edge of his thoughts. Strange One could not name it, for it was entangled with pride. He had a vague feeling that it involved Ruthe's pretty cords.

Chapter 23

I can hardly wait to leave this evil place.

The clatter of dragons woke her. Gwendolyn winced at the complaints of her tight muscles and sunburned skin. She crawled to the front of her crevice.

The young dragons circled the she-dragon. "Mother, we're hungry! We only had that awful bachelor's button."

Gwendolyn smiled. *Pigs don't like that weed either. And all children have tantrums when they're hungry. What will the she-dragon feed her children?*

"My throat burns!" another young dragon complained.

"One day of hunger won't hurt you," said the she-dragon. "I don't want to catch any of you eating anything today." She glanced at each one to make sure they understood she was serious.

"You said last night was going to be special." The largest of the young dragons challenged his mother. "What's so special about those weeds anyway?"

"You do not question me!" the she-dragon shrieked.

The youngster stood his ground with his jaw jutting out defiantly. She cuffed him. He still did not step back, and the she-dragon almost imperceptibly nodded approval.

Then she continued, "Now I want to look at each of your throats."

"Why, Mother?" questioned a young female.

"Because I said so!"

The brood fell silent, and Gwendolyn watched, immobilized. The young dragons sullenly opened their mouths. After she had checked several throats, the mother murmured, "Good, good—warm glows in all their throats." Even Gwendolyn felt relieved.

However, the smallest of the dragons did not pass her inspection.

"Idiot! you didn't eat enough of the bachelor's button. Your throat is as cold as a metal sword. Tonight you will fly back and eat until you are stuffed. And when you have done as I have ordered, I want you to remember this."

With those words, the she-dragon hit her child. He fell to his knees.

Gwendolyn watched in shock.

The young dragon got to his feet fighting to keep tears from spilling from his eyes. None of the others offered any comfort.

"Tonight remember the hurt of the slap . . ." the she-dragon continued, "and the sting of my words. You are an embarrassment. I trust you are, however, dragon enough to avoid feeling sorry for yourself. Of course, I might be wrong."

The wetness in the young dragon's eyes dried into defiance and anger. Again the she-dragon's face fleetingly registered approval, but she only said, "We will see if you have a dragon's memory for grudges or if you are indeed only a large lizard."

She then sent her sons to a corner to play amongst themselves. She promised that the winner would receive a jewel while the losers would each forfeit a coin.

Gwendolyn watched in horror as the young males butted, bit, and ripped at each other. She could see no playfulness between them.

The she-dragon led her two daughters away from the males and nearer Gwendolyn's crevice. Gwendolyn stilled her every twitch and breathed as shallowly and quietly as possible.

"What I tell you now," began the she-dragon, "I will tell you this one time only. If you forget, dragon secrets and power will be lost in your line. Shame will be on your head, and your children will be weak.

"Dragons are the most feared of all creatures. Do you know why?"

"Because we never forget who we are," answered the young female with fire in her eyes.

"Never," agreed her mother. "From the moment of hatching, dragons are raised fierce and proud. Other creatures, even bears and wolves, have a softness for their young. If you are ever tempted to show love or understanding for your children, you will weaken them; you will undermine their preparation for dragon life; and you will corrupt our line. Your children will relax their guard when they should be ready for battle. Do you grasp this?"

The two young females nodded their heads in understanding and agreement. Gwendolyn flinched at the harsh words.

"You will never best your brothers in strength or size," the mother continued, "but I will give you the knowledge and power that make you their equals. You will carry the knowledge of fire and will pass the fire to your children."

Gwendolyn could hardly believe her good fortune. She closed her eyes to focus attention on the she-dragon's words.

"But we don't have fire yet, Mother," whined the second female.

"Be quiet and listen," the she-dragon snarled. "You are so stupid."

Startled, Gwendolyn opened her eyes. She saw the males looking at their sister and gloating at her discomfort.

The she-dragon lowered her voice again, and Gwendolyn readied herself to memorize every word. "Names of power contain the essence of a being. To know a being's true name is to hold invisible power. Never give the power I'm about to give you to your brothers, or they will have both their strength and your power to name the weed.

"You will give fire to both your sons and daughters," continued the she-dragon, "but the name only to your daughters. The weed you ate last night is also called feverfew. There is fire in the naming.

"When your hatchlings eat the weed, you must say to yourself only,

> 'Powers of the dragon—
> Secrets, fire, and gold.
> Fire flames from feverfew
> Only when the name be told.'

"Remember, the power of the true name is needed to bestow the power of the weed and part of the bestowing of dragon's fire and terror—your fire and terror," she finished.

"A part of getting our fire? Mother, what's the rest?"

Yes, echoed Gwendolyn silently. *What's the rest?*

"Watch me tonight, and you will know what to do. You will know the rest when your fire flames. If you have truly learned all I have taught you, you will know how to give your children fire. Shush! your brother is coming."

The runt male, who was smaller than either of his sisters, whimpered as he approached, "Mother, he really hurt me." The small dragon bled from a deep bite, and a portion of one leathery wing was ripped.

"Crybaby," taunted the young female who had previously earned her mother's ire. "Rek is a...." The look from the she-dragon stopped her in mid-sentence.

"Worse than a cry-baby is a name-loser!" bellowed the mother dragon. "You are never to reveal the names of your brothers or sister. You are never to say their names aloud. To speak a hatch-mate's name is to betray and to receive betrayal in return. If anyone of you ever loses another's name, we will chant your name for all to hear.

"You must never let anyone who is not a brood mate know your name. You must also have a riddle for your name. It is the most important riddle of your life. It must be impossible for another dragon to guess. The second most important riddle of your life is one you can solve to correctly guess another dragon's name. Do that, and you will acquire great power.

"Now, I will have two coins from a crybaby and all the jewels from a name-loser. And you . . .," the she-dragon indicated the female, "you will fly with your brother tonight. When he eats the bachelor's buttons, you will do what has just been explained to you. Understand?"

The young female looked down and nodded.

Then the mother looked over to judge the fight among her sons. The largest one clearly held the other male at bay. She mouthed a nearby ruby and tossed it to the winner.

"I want a coin—make that two coins—from each of the losers." She turned to the runt, "That's four coins from you—two for crying and two for losing. Now all of you, leave me alone. I want to sleep."

The young dragons slipped into their individual compartments. Some returned with the payment from their meager treasures, dropped their offerings, and went back to their chambers.

Gwendolyn shook her head. *Those creatures only touch cold jewels and metal. They don't love each other at all—not even their mother— especially not her! I can hardly wait to leave this evil place, but I must watch the she-dragon tonight.*

Feverfew. Bachelor's button is also called feverfew. There's some growing close to the stable. Strange One isn't a fighter, but he will have the knowledge of the naming. She practiced the chant so she would not forget.

I'm so glad I found Strange One's egg. He is much too sensitive and loving to be raised by a creature like this she-dragon. The pig shifted position. *Ow, everything hurts. I'll leave as soon as they go tonight. I hope the moon is bright enough to show me the markers.* The thought of finding the markers and then the stream reminded her how thirsty and hungry she was. The day seemed to last forever.

Finally, the young dragons roused and came out of their chambers to join the she-dragon in the big tunnel.

"What shall we do tonight, Mother? We'll hunt, right?"

"I'm so hungry, I could eat four horses!"

"I smell something funny."

"That's just the fev . . ." the young female caught herself, "the bachelor's button on our breath."

"No, it's different. It's something to eat."

Gwendolyn held her breath. *Should I have tried to leave while the dragons slept? If they find me, they can't reach me. But they could trap me here until I starve. Or would the she- dragon cook me with her flames?*

"Idiot!" said the intense young female in a tone like her mother's, "you just think you smell food because you're hungry."

"Well, where will we hunt then?" he responded.

Gwendolyn exhaled.

The she-dragon finally spoke. "I don't know where you'll hunt. As of now, you're on your own. Leave my cave and don't return."

For a moment, all was still as the young dragons stood in shock.

The largest found his courage first. "Leave? This is our home."

"No, this is my cave, and I don't expect to see you again until the gathering."

"What gathering?" several asked at once.

"You are all such stupid dragons. I don't know how I've put up with you for so long. Once in every cycle of seasons, on the first full moon after day and night are equal and the air begins to chill, the dragons gather for contests and feasting. The she-dragons present their broods. That is when you must have a riddle for your name.

And, other than keeping the secret of each other's names, that is the last time you will have a family.

"Look to the moon and to the circling dragons. I'm angered you don't remember this," she concluded and sat for a silent moment.

"We didn't forget. You never told us," accused one of the females with a small burst of flame.

"You never said we had to leave!'" Another belched a scorching accusation.

"Well, you do," the she-dragon answered with infuriating calm. "Go, find your own cave . . . if you can. You may each take one piece of your treasure with you, and I'd say that was generous."

"One piece!" The cave was a mass of furious dragons. Blind with fury, they circled the large chamber. Flames shot out ever farther from all but the runt.

The cool damp of the cave warmed and dried. Acrid smoke filled the air, and Gwendolyn stifled her urge to cough.

"Go!" screamed the she-dragon. "Go!"

As the young dragons took a piece of treasure, they each, except for the runt, spat a flame of hatred at the she-dragon.

Gwendolyn watched motionless, stunned by the cruelty. "I must leave this evil, evil hole," she whispered.

The heat subsided, and only the she-dragon remained. She gazed around the cave, almost longingly it seemed to Gwendolyn.

"Rid of those monsters at last. I'll not miss them, oh, no. And next year there will be another batch to try my patience."

Is that sorrow in her voice? Sorrow after all the horrible things she said? I don't understand.

The dragon lumbered out of the cave.

As soon as Gwendolyn heard the last flap of powerful wings, she raced out to the ledge and down the summit.

CHAPTER 24

None of the dragons were kind.

D uck flew overhead and shouted, "She's almost home!" Strange One and the piglets all dashed to the fence. Tails wagged and feet pranced.

The farmer hammered the last nail in the gate and looked up. "Ruthe," he called, "your fool pig's come back." He herded Gwendolyn through the opening and fastened the gate behind her.

The piglets, all asking questions at the same time, encircled Gwendolyn.

Duck pushed her way in. "Sit down and listen," she ordered.

Strange One wanted to touch Gwendolyn to make sure she was real. He had questions too, but he didn't want anyone else to hear them.

Finally, the piglets quieted. Gwendolyn told them about her journey, being chased by a wolf, and hiding in the dragon's cave.

Duck looked at Gwendolyn with admiration, "I didn't know you were so brave."

I didn't either, Strange One thought.

"I'm not," Gwendolyn said, "I almost came back home many times, and I hid whenever I had the chance. But I was more afraid that, if I gave up, I wouldn't be a good mother."

Table Scraps sang:

> "My mama got away from a wolf.
> Oh, she tricked him good.
> She hid in a dragon cave—
> Heard them talk and she didn't get caught.
> My mama got away!"

"Wait until the chickens hear about what Mama did!" Sweet Pea boasted.

Nasturtium chimed in, "And wait until Mama hears how Strange One saved the chickens!"

Gwendolyn looked at Strange One and knit her brows with a question.

He cast his gaze downward. He didn't want to talk about the fox and the chickens until he could ask about the eggs. Finally he looked back up into Gwendolyn's eyes and asked, "What are the dragons like? Did you find out about fire?"

"Feverfew!" Gwendolyn exclaimed. "We need bachelor's button for your fire, Strange One. Duck, will you get some for us?"

"Never met a pig who needed so much help," the bird groused before she flew over the fence to a patch of the weed that grew along with wild oats. She grunted as she pulled out plants one by one. Then she carried them back over the fence.

"Phooey!" Duck spat out the bachelor's button.

I'm not eating that.

Gwendolyn nosed the plants to the dragon. He sniffed, wrinkled his nose, and frowned.

"I hate plants. And remember, your idea about the candle didn't work. I burned my mouth and didn't get fire anyway."

"I agree that was a bad idea. But now we know that dragons eat feverfew."

"Feverfew? These are bachelor's buttons—not feverfew! It's

stupid to think a plant will let me breathe fire—especially if it isn't even the right plant."

"The plant has two names," Gwendolyn responded, "and only the female dragons know the name feverfew. Don't forget it."

"I'm a male. So why do I have to know the name?" *Mama is saying things that just get more ridiculous all the time.*

"I don't understand all of it. The males have some powers that the females don't, and the females have the power of naming. Names are very important to dragons. Anyway, both the males and females will be able to breathe fire, but only females get the name and the words that will let young dragons first acquire their fire. So if you remember the name and the words, you'll have both your male power and the female kinds of power." Gwendolyn smiled. "Isn't that great! So go ahead. Eat the feverfew."

Strange One sat without making a move towards the plants. "Do dragons like feverfew?" he asked.

"Well, no," Gwendolyn answered, "they didn't, but they ate it. Please, Strange One. If it doesn't work, we won't try anything else."

"Hey," said Table Scraps, "if Duck gets more plants, maybe I can breathe fire too!"

"Your throat is different than Strange One's. It won't work for you."

"Besides that, I'm not getting any more. Phooey!" added Duck.

Gwendolyn turned her attention back to Strange One. He sniffed the plants and made a face.

"All of them," the pig prodded. "One dragon had to go back and eat some more. And you need to memorize these words:

"Powers of the dragon—
Secrets, fire, and gold.
Fire flames from feverfew
Only when the name be told."

Reluctantly, Strange One choked down the leaves. He tried to remember the words instead of thinking about how bad the plants tasted.

"On my way back to the farm," Gwendolyn continued, "I made up some words too, just for you:

"Powers of my dragon—
Love, fire, and flight.
Loving starts with family
And holds us with its might."

Seven and Table Scraps laughed. Strange One coughed on his last swallow.

"Open up," Gwendolyn ordered.

The dragon slowly spread his jaws half way open.

"Wider," said the pig. "I can't see your throat yet."

Who says I want you to? Strange One opened his jaws slightly farther.

"The she-dragon looked for a rosy glow," Gwendolyn explained. "I don't see anything. But wait, the glow wasn't until the next day, and the dragons didn't get anything to eat or drink. So don't drink any water or eat tonight."

"Not all night?"

"Maybe longer."

Strange One couldn't remember ever feeling so irritated with Mama before. He should be able to decide for himself if he wanted to breathe fire or not.

"Don't eat or drink any water," Gwendolyn repeated. "Promise me."

Strange One sighed. "Mama, what are the powers only the males have?" he asked.

"They are bigger and stronger, and they fight," she answered bluntly.

"The males are mean, aren't they? Am . . . Will I grow up to be mean too?"

"What do you mean 'will'?" Table Scraps teased. "Ow! Duck, why did you bite me?"

"No, you will not be a mean dragon. You are kind, loving and . . ." Gwendolyn glared at Table Scraps, "more sensitive than many pigs.

"None of the dragons were kind to each other, Strange One, not just the males. I don't know why the she-dragon didn't teach them to get along. She gave gold to the one that fought the best.

"One dragon named Rek had his wing torn badly when the males played together, and the she-dragon just said cruel things to him. The one good thing is that the dragons only gather one night a year. So maybe it doesn't really matter if they get along or not."

It matters to me. It matters a lot . . . And Table Scraps sure doesn't envy me now.

Secrets of the Flame

Chapter 25

Just in time for what?

Gwendolyn awoke the next morning brimming with happiness. How good to sleep surrounded by the warmth of her family again. She looked with love at her still-sleeping children. *I can hardly wait to check Strange One's throat . . . and his mood. He was so argumentative yesterday—argumentative and sad.* She took a deep breath. *Harvest is in the air.*

The piglets stirred and rose. Strange One groggily lifted an eyelid.

Gwendolyn thought of the cave dragons' habits. *I never paid attention before. Strange One is almost always the last one to fall asleep and the last one to wake up. Maybe that's the dragon in him.*

When Strange One yawned and stretched, Gwendolyn could see a glow in the back of his throat.

"The feverfew made your throat rosy! Let's see if you can breathe fire," she urged.

The whole family pushed outside. The piglets jostled for a good position.

"Piglets, stand back. Do you want your snouts scorched? Strange One, don't face anything that can burn."

Secrets of the Flame

"What do I do?"

"Just open your mouth and blow out fire, I guess." Gwendolyn quivered with excitement. *If Strange One breathes fire, it's worth almost getting eaten. Will the farmer be pleased? Will Strange One?*

The piglets watched wide-eyed as Strange One opened his jaws, took a deep breath and huffed mightily.

Nothing happened.

Gwendolyn looked at his throat again. "The glow is definitely there. At least you didn't blow it out."

"My throat burns like it did after I ate the candle. Why doesn't it work?"

"Try again," she said.

No flame. Not even a spark flew from the dragon's mouth.

What am I missing? Gwendolyn remembered the rest of the she-dragon's words. "There's one more thing," she said.

"What?" Strange One and some of the piglets asked

"I don't know. The she-dragon told the females they should pay attention and they would understand the last part of what they'll need to do for their children to get fire.

"But I didn't see or hear anything that tells me what she meant. The dragons got up to hunt, and the she-dragon told them they couldn't live there anymore. All the young dragons got mad, and whoosh—a cave full of fire-breathing dragons.

"Maybe the she-dragon said some more secret words," Gwendolyn mused, "and then when everybody got so mad, she didn't get a chance to tell the females about the last part. Maybe that was why the she-dragon seemed sad after her children left."

Gwendolyn sighed. "I'm so sorry, Strange One." Her voice wavered. "I failed."

The piglets all grumbled. "Now we'll never see a fire-breathing dragon, ever," said Table Scraps. "Strange One, are you sure you tried hard enough?"

"Yeah," echoed Onion, "are you sure you tried hard enough? We want to see a fire-breathing dragon!"

Then Sweet Pea, Buttercup, and Truffle joined in a chant, "Fire! Fire! Fire!"

Strange One appeared both embarrassed and annoyed. "Fire," he scoffed. "Who needs fire? The humans already found a way for me to be useful. I don't need to have fire. Ruthe's making me . . ."

"What? Why didn't you tell me yesterday?" Gwendolyn interrupted. *The humans found a reason to keep my child. Strange One won't have to leave the farm!* "What way to be useful?

"I . . . we don't know," Strange One answered. "But Ruthe is making me something pretty to wear. She comes with it everyday."

Gwendolyn's forehead wrinkled—*something pretty to wear?*

"What is it?" she asked.

"I don't know. But it has long cords with different colors twisted together and it fits around my head. I think she's even going to decorate it with flowers when it's finished."

"With a lot of pretty colors!" Buttercup pouted, "Why does Strange One get everything special?"

Truffle was hopeful, "I think she'll make one for each of us after she finishes the one for Strange One."

"Yeah," agreed Seven, "and I want purple in mine."

It didn't make sense to Gwendolyn, but the problem was solved. "Maybe it's just as well you can't breathe fire."

The gate creaked when Ruthe opened and shut it again. She carried multicolored cords draped around her neck and went first to Gwendolyn.

"I knew you'd come back." Ruthe patted the pig's side and scratched her jowls. "Sometimes I've wanted to go exploring too. But I knew you wouldn't leave your young ones forever.

"Here, look at what I'm making for your dragon." The woman stretched out the cords. "Of course, you can't really tell how it looks until I put it on him." Ruthe stood beside the dragon and stroked his neck in a calming gesture. "Time to try on your halter."

Gwendolyn didn't recognize the word. Ruthe arranged the cords. *That looks like the binding the humans put on the horse or the cows when they want to ride or lead them. Why do the humans want Strange One to have them too? I guess it doesn't matter as long as Strange One can stay. That's all I need to know.*

Ruthe stepped back. "Looks fine on him, it does indeed. It should be finished by tomorrow and just in time."

Just in time for what? Gwendolyn longed for human speech to ask her friend, *Just in time for what?*

The human took the cords off Strange One. She patted Gwendolyn again and said, "It's so good to have you back, dear Gwen. And we will all be so proud of your dragon!" The gate creaked as Ruthe left the pen.

Just in time for what to make us all proud? And why doesn't this feel right.

Chapter 26

I want to fly free.

Strange One sulked. The piglets were still disappointed they didn't get to see him blow fire. *Mama gets everybody's hopes up, and then, when her idea doesn't work, who gets blamed? Me! And I never even wanted to eat the candle or the feverfew. It just isn't fair!*

The day passed slowly. Buttercup and Onion conversed with the chickens. Gwendolyn watched with a displeased expression. The other piglets rooted along the edge of the fence.

Strange One sat by himself and felt ignored. The humans seemed to be bustling around more than usual, but maybe it only seemed more than usual because the dragon was so bored and annoyed with everything.

Finally, Strange One walked over to Gwendolyn and sat.

"Mama, remember when we told you how I killed the fox and saved the chickens?"

Gwendolyn nodded, and Strange One continued, "And the farmer gave me the fox to eat? Well, that's not all. I ate two eggs. I don't know why the chickens got so mad. The humans eat their eggs all the time, and the two I ate weren't even in nests.

"The chickens called me a murderer and a cannibal. Is it wrong to eat eggs, but alright to eat foxes? What about rabbits? I don't understand what I can eat, and you weren't here to help!" *There, I said it!*

Gwendolyn's mouth hung open. She finally seemed to find her voice. "Of course you're not a murderer or a cannibal. Eggs aren't farm animals. You would never, ever, eat a farm animal, right? That would be wrong, wrong, wrong! Fish are acceptable. Duck eats them sometimes. I don't know about rabbits or other animals. Maybe you shouldn't eat anything with fur."

"But the farmer gave me the fox after he took the fur off. I started to worry that the fox had babies to feed."

"The human is coming!" shouted Sweet Pea. Then he slumped. "But she doesn't have the bucket—just Strange One's cords."

"The halter is finished," Ruthe announced. "Isn't it beautiful and just in time too." She calmly approached Strange One while speaking in a soothing tone. "The lord's tax collector will be here any day to measure our harvest and take the lord's share. A tame dragon will make a fine gift for the lord."

I'm not a gift. Strange One took a step back.

Ruthe's gentle words and movements continued. "In exchange for such an unusual and rare gift, perhaps the lord will reward us. Perhaps he will collect no taxes this year."

Strange One moved farther away. *What is she talking about?*

"We think, the lord, in turn, will give this magnificent dragon to the king. A proud and noble king such as ours would surely be pleased. Just imagine, a king riding our dragon! His enemies would think twice before challenging him."

Strange One stopped moving away. *Ride into battle with a king on my back?*

"Then the king," Ruthe went on, "may smile with favor on the lord who gave him such a gift, and the lord will, in turn, find much favor with his peasants." Ruthe smiled warmly at Gwendolyn. "And my husband will appreciate his adventurous pig."

Ruthe reached toward Strange One's head.

Battles sound exciting. But what does it mean that I would be a gift? Would the king own me? Does that mean I could only go where he said? Strange One ducked.

"This won't hurt," Ruthe assured him. "And a dragon that is mount to a king will have fine, jeweled bridles and saddles. How grand you will look. You will eat royal food and sleep in a well-appointed barn."

Strange One dodged the halter, and Ruthe dropped it to her side.

"You don't understand what I'm saying, do you, dragon? I'll just slip this on when I bring food later. Then you can get used to wearing it." With that Ruthe left the pen and returned to the cottage.

Gwendolyn beamed. "Strange One, you could carry the king! You will have all the food you need, and a barn so large you will never outgrow it. Oh, I'll miss you so much. I hoped we could all stay here. But you will be safe and well-cared for. This is all going to work out!"

Strange One did not agree. The humans' plans for him felt like a tight prison. *I don't want my life to be just what Mama or the humans think it should be.*

Strange One felt as if the edge of everything he knew was cracking. *There's more. I don't know what it is, but there's more out there.*

"I want to fly," he said.

"Oh, I'm sure you will," Gwendolyn said. "And you won't have to worry about finding all your own food or getting fire. This is the best thing that could happen."

"No," countered Strange One, "I don't want to be harnessed and tied so I can never go my own way. I want to fly free, like Duck and those robins you told me to copy. I . . . I want to see other dragons for myself!"

Chapter 27

Her heart felt as hollow as a gourd.

"But you'll be safe if you belong to the king. You're going with the tax collector," Gwendolyn insisted. "I've seen how dangerous the wild world and dragons are. I don't want you to take those chances. Remember, you don't have fire to protect yourself."

"Mama, you went to find the dragons, and you didn't have fire. You outsmarted a wolf. If you don't want me to go to the wilds, does that mean you're sorry you did?"

"That was different. I was coming back." *Why doesn't Strange One see reason?*

"Mama," pushed Nasturtium, "are you sorry you went? You went to get fire for Strange One, but you didn't. Are you sorry you went?"

"No," Gwendolyn whispered, sure she was giving Strange One his next argument.

"Mama," Nasturtium persisted, "you're not sorry and you're not even a dragon. Maybe Strange One won't be sorry either. And maybe he would hate belonging to a king."

Gwendolyn could barely choke out the words, "But I won't know if he's all right or even if he's alive."

"We didn't know if you were alive or not," snapped Strange One. "All we knew was that if you didn't come back soon, you never would."

Nasturtium interceded again. She stood close to Gwendolyn and nuzzled the pig's face. "We'll all miss Strange One, Mama, and we'll wonder how he is, no matter where he goes."

Gwendolyn struggled to calm her breathing. *I'm glad I went on my quest even I didn't find all the secrets of fire. I discovered I'm braver and cleverer than I thought. I had one real adventure.*

But this is my child . . . who is no longer a child.

"I'm going to fly free!" Strange One asserted.

In that instant, Gwendolyn understood she could not decide for Strange One. *All I can decide is if he goes with or without my blessing.*

"There's not much time then, so listen carefully." Gwendolyn moved closer to Strange One. The piglets formed a circle around their mother and brother.

"Fly to the mountains and find a cave."

"I know to do that, Mama." Strange One stomped his foot in impatience.

"The days are getting shorter. If you want to find the dragons, mark when the day and night are equal. And, at the next full moon, look to the night sky. The dragons will gather, but I don't know where. Be cautious. You don't have to join them. Just look and listen, learn what you can. Remember how the dragons hurt that little dragon Rek, and he's their brother.

"Also don't forget . . ."

"I know, Mama."

Table Scraps yelled, "The humans are coming!"

"Strange One, we love you. Remember, you are not a dragon-like dragon." Gwendolyn rushed to get in the most important words. "Please come back."

The pig looked to the humans who seemed to sense they should hurry. The dragon still did not take off.

"Strange One," Gwendolyn shouted, "fly now!" She ducked and pushed the piglets back as her child's wings unfurled and pumped down mightily. The farmer tried to throw the halter over Strange One's head and neck, but the colorful cords bounced and slid off as the the dragon left the ground.

Gwendolyn choked back a sob. Strange One was gone. Her heart felt as hollow as a gourd.

Chapter 28

I honestly won't hurt you.

It was harder to leave than Strange One anticipated. Gwendolyn's shout and the sight of the humans finally propelled him upward over fields of golden flax and toward the mountains. His wings beat the air with the strength of a powerful anger that masked his other emotions.

Why does Mama think I need a king to take care of me? Why does she always think she has to tell me everything and to teach me to think like a pig? How could she ever trust those humans? She is stupider than the chickens! One question he could not form into words. Why hadn't she tried harder to change his mind?

Strange One flew on and on, farther than he had ever gone before. His muscles grew tired until he could no longer sustain the anger as a shield from fearfulness and doubts. *Did I make the right choice? If I find other dragons, what will they do to me? Will I always be alone now?*

His wings slowed as sorrow washed through him like a torrent in a canyon. It finally ebbed and left behind a stronger will than Strange One had known he possessed.

"I'll take care of myself and make my own choices!"

Strange One flew past mountainsides with scorched, lifeless patches, the signs of dragon territory. He flew deeper into the mountains until he found a high slope with no signs of any dragons. He circled it from top to bottom. *I'll be safe here. What's that? Looks like a cave opening below the tree line. Hard to see. Nobody will find me if I don't want them to.*

Strange One pulled his head and neck back, thrust his hind feet forward, and used his wings to slow his speed. The landing was best suited for touching down on flat ground. It was awkward but workable on the incline of the mountain. He walked through the oaks toward the cave.

The closer he got, the more his excitement rose. "It looks big enough and nothing's been burned. It doesn't look like any other kind of animal lives here either. Oh, I hope . . ."

Strange One crept in and found a space with enough room to turn around. He peered out at the darkening sky. Off in the distance the shape of a lone dragon circled. The solitary figure dived and disappeared from view. *Hunting.* Strange One shivered at the thought of Gwendolyn's journey and wriggled back into the cave.

Time to see just how big this cave is.

The nearly straight tunnel opened up into a wider room. By the moonlight that dimly lit the chamber, Strange One's cat-like eyes saw three smaller tunnels leading off the main room.

"Hello," the dragon called. He heard no answer except for the echo. *I have a home.* Strange One circled round and round to somehow create a sleeping spot that would not, for the first time in his life, be warmed by his family.

※ ※ ※

When Strange One woke, he examined his cave more carefully. Rocks jutted from packed earthen walls, and flecks of minerals glinted in the dim light. A purple sparkle caught his attention, and he walked closer to investigate. Clinging to a drab, gray rock was a translucent rock with many flat smooth sides. When Strange One moved his head just so, he could see tiny rainbows.

"A crystal! My cave has a crystal!"

The dragon poked his head down each of the three smaller tunnels, but his body was too big to fit into any of them.

A pig could go in. I wish Table Scraps and Nasturtium and the others were here to see. If they were, this would be perfect.

Strange One's stomach rumbled, a reminder he hadn't eaten the night before.

He noticed sounds from outside. The yammering of a mockingbird. Scratches and scrambles. *Probably squirrels or mice.* Two thoughts flew through his mind so quickly he wasn't sure which one came first or foremost. *I wonder what forest animals talk about. I wonder what they taste like.*

"I don't know whether those animals are friends or food. I need both. Stupid pig, you didn't know anything about how to raise a dragon. You didn't teach me anything important. Duck would have been a better mother for me!"

He hollered out of the cave, "Don't worry, Mockingbird. I won't eat you. I'll never eat a bird. But watch out . . ."

Watch out, what? Watch out, slugs? Strange One couldn't help himself. He laughed. *Watch out, fish? Yes, I'll eat fish, lizards, and . . .* he would have to think about this some more.

And friends? I don't have any friends anymore. I'm alone. I just promised the mockingbird I won't eat birds. So I'll try to make friends with some birds and some . . . he would have to think about this some more too.

The calls and rustlings from outside started up again while the dragon was thinking.

When he walked out of his cave, the sounds stopped. In the silence, Strange One made a decision. *I won't hunt close to the cave. Every animal near my cave, even a slug, is safe.*

"I honestly won't hurt you," he called out. "I'd really like to talk to someone . . . please."

The mountain's only answer was the sound of swaying leaves.

CHAPTER 29

She would need more bravery now.

Gwendolyn felt a gaping hole even though the stable and now the fenced area were too crowded. She paced the pen's perimeter and scanned the sky. She squinted at the forest beyond the fields. At the end of the day, her eyes burned, her head throbbed, and her neck and hooves ached.

Strange One made my world bigger than I could imagine. And now, everything on the farm feels too tight and too empty at the same time.

"If I could only know that he's safe," she fretted. "If I could just see he's happy with his decision, that would be enough."

One day she mentioned an idea to Duck, "What do you think about another journey? This one wouldn't be dangerous. It would be to find Strange One."

Duck rolled her eyes. "Come, Pig, every child leaves the nest. You're acting like a fussing hen. You're all aflutter, but a child leaving is just part of our cycle."

"I realize Strange One had to leave, Duck. You needn't act so superior. It's just that I can't seem to feel settled until I know he is safe. If I went looking, I could just check on him. Perhaps I could help, if he was in trouble."

Duck sat unmoved.

"I wouldn't even have to let him know I was there," Gwendolyn continued. "I'd feel reassured. Of course, it would be easier to find him from the sky . . . if someone would help me look."

Duck stared. "Pig, I sat and warmed your egg. I taught your hatchling to find food and fly. I even fetched feverfew for your hare-brained plan to make Strange One into a fire-breathing dragon. But I won't help you rescue him from his own life. Besides, you still have other children. Fuss over them." She clamped her bill shut.

"It's not as if I've ignored the piglets!" Gwendolyn snapped. She turned away and pretended not to hear Duck's hiss.

How can I love a child and then just forget him? It wasn't really a question in her mind. It was an impossibility. When the pig decided to mother the baby dragon, she hadn't known how much of her heart he would fill. She hadn't known that she would need more bravery now than she needed when she hid in a dragon cave.

After Strange One left, Gwendolyn had thrown herself into teaching the piglets everything they needed to learn, only to discover they already knew.

But the piglets did have questions—questions about things beyond the farm. Were there other pigs? Since Strange One left the farm, would they leave too?

They're not worried about Strange One. They're envious!

Chapter 30

We will first introduce the young dragons.

Strange One's days took on a pattern. He rose later and later each day until he gradually became nocturnal. He left the cave at dusk to fish and drink. He looked for shiny rocks to collect for treasure. At dawn, he returned to his cave.

The same two issues haunted him—food and friends. He needed both, though he feared he could only have one. He had to eat, and fish were not always plentiful. In areas far from his cave, he reluctantly began to hunt for small animals such as squirrels. He watched other creatures whenever he could, but none ever talked with him.

One dusk he wandered to the lake still trying to puzzle it all out. *Wild animals have to search for what they eat. A mouse finds seeds, and a snake might eat the mouse. A fox could eat the snake or another mouse. So a mouse is afraid of all kinds of animals. A snake isn't afraid of mice, but it has to hide from foxes, wolves, and hawks. I don't know of any animal that hunts a wolf. But when a wolf dies, a vulture might eat it, and for sure, little maggots and other insects will. Mice probably eat maggots.*

"It's all connected!" Strange One exclaimed. "This goes around and around. I'm part of it too!" *But I still don't know if there are rules about which animals I shouldn't eat. Mama thought no farm animals. Does that mean all other animals are okay? I felt really bad when I worried about the fox's babies. How do I decide?*

And how do I find friends? Even though maggots eat everything, including the very biggest and strongest animals, nobody is afraid of them. But every animal is afraid of me just because I'm so big.

"Mama and Duck were really brave to take care of me and let me be friends with the piglets and ducklings," he admitted. *Maybe I'll never have friends again.*

Strange One became aware of the evening sounds—slow cricket chirps, birds rustling in trees, an owl's hoot.

He looked at the night sky and realized the days were growing a bit shorter. *It's past the time the day and night are equal.*

There's one place I might find friends—the dragon gathering.

He checked the moon. *It looks almost full but not quite. Tomorrow night . . . I'm going!*

Strange One's thoughts circled. *Someone to talk to! I can to tell them about my cave and my crystal. I can ask questions, hear stories and riddles. Maybe . . .*

Maybe they'll find out I don't have fire. Will they want to fight? Will they accept me at all?

All I know for certain is they won't be afraid of me. The dragons might be kind or, more likely, mean; but they won't be afraid. I'm going to risk it. I can hide behind trees or rocks, at least at first.

And if I can't find a place to hide, I'll hide in the open, hide by acting like everyone else. I won't look different from everyone else!

A sensation of tightness and of edges about to crack somehow felt familiar to him. He sensed a promise of finding something more than the everything he knew.

※※※

The next evening, Strange One scanned the heavens. The light drained from the sky. A faint star twinkled. To the east, the first curve of the moon peeked over the horizon. As the sky darkened, the full moon rose and shone more brightly. Soon Strange One spotted a moving speck that grew until he could make out the shape of a dragon.

When the dragon was overhead, Strange One automatically ducked, but checked his impulse to hide in the cave. He watched the sky gradually fill with dragons who converged from all directions to a spot over the tallest peak in the mountain range. Once there, they joined an enormous ring of gliding dragons that spiraled downward. Strange One marveled at the dazzling display and quivered in anticipation.

"Slowly and quickly; quickly and slowly," he chanted calming words and took to the sky.

Once aloft, he flew with his head low and his neck straight. Each strong flap of his wings carried him closer to the ring of circling dragons. Strange One could see that the other dragons elevated and arched their necks when they got close to the swirling ring. He tried to imitate their style and struggled to pull his head up. His neck wobbled. He put his head straight ahead as Duck had taught him.

This is no time to relearn how to fly. But now I know why a dragon shouldn't learn flying from a duck. I'm going to have to try to land the same way the others do or they'll know I'm an outsider.

When he reached the peak, Strange One dipped one wing and coasted into the spiral. He tipped further and pulled the spirals tighter as he descended. On the last loop, he straightened himself; and, instead of circling one more time before landing in the midst of the crowd, he dropped to the ground behind a stand of trees where he faded into the shadows.

Strange One watched as dragons formed themselves into rows facing the largest, most imposing dragon of all. This dragon's metallic-red body glowed in the moonlight. A tuft of silvery hair sprouted from his chin. His eyes glowered and burned as he scanned the congregation and stared at the most ferocious looking dragon.

When the leader cleared his throat, all talking, all shuffling, all sounds immediately ceased.

"I bid welcome to you of lesser power, to those of you who join here for the first time, and to those of you who aspire to my position."

"Hail to our strongest, elder leader," the dragons responded.

Strange One noticed a large blue male spit out the greeting and stare defiantly at the leader, who calmly returned the ominous expression.

"As is our custom," the leader continued, "we will first introduce the young dragons. Of these weak ones, some will, in later years, be of importance to our kind. One of these may even someday challenge and hold the leader's position. She-dragons, gather your broods and present those who have survived the first moon cycle on their own— those who are therefore not the weakest of the weak."

Several full-grown females moved to the front and were joined by clusters of younger dragons who were about the same size as Strange One. Almost all of the young dragons were shades of green. A few were bronze.

"We're the youngest ones here at our first gathering," he whispered to himself. He did not feel quite so alone.

Some of the young dragons swaggered in front of the leader. Others tried to hide behind their mothers. The mothers snapped in annoyance at their timid youngsters and prodded them forward.

Strange One stared at one fearful dragon with a tear in one wing. The edges of the tear showed healing but hadn't mended together. A portion of the wing flapped in tatters. And a white scar against the dull green of his hindquarters clearly revealed the marks of dragon teeth.

The leader eyed the cautious young ones with disdain. He continued, "You are each to present a riddle about your name. If any dragon correctly guesses, you will be in service to that dragon until the next gathering. Is that understood?

"I usually have several young to do my bidding, so choose your words carefully. There is only one rule, a hatch-mate cannot answer or give away the name of a brother or a sister. To do so results in banishment from all dragon gatherings forever."

"Revere the power of the name," chanted the gathering.

Strange One breathed a sigh of relief. *It's good thing I hid since I don't have a litter, I mean a brood, to join and I never made up a riddle about my name. I can't do anything about not having a mother or hatch-mates. But I can try to make up a riddle, just in case.*

"Now for the riddling! You, weak kitten," the leader smiled with malevolence and indicated a small dragon who was trying to hide behind her family, "what is your riddle?"

The young one barely managed to speak. "Delight kept from light," she stammered. "Buried in cavern, not covered."

"So obvious," scoffed the leader. "Dragon's Treasure, you are mine. She-dragons take note. Coddled young cannot fight or confound. Kindness begets only incompetence."

The young dragon and her mother both hung their heads in shame as the youngster reluctantly plodded to the rear of the enormous leader, who scanned the gathering.

"I know I don't need to remind you of the penalty for an erroneous guess." He looked his prize over, giving the crowd time to note his self-confidence.

The next young dragon was prepared. The crowd appreciated the clever riddle, but no one tried to guess her name. Strange One watched the ritual in fascination. Although he didn't intend to join the gathering, he puzzled over the riddles just the same. He noticed that some protected themselves with nonsense riddles that gave no real clues. They earned the crowd's disapproval. But the gathering praised the young dragons who made up difficult riddles that left the listeners puzzling over possible answers.

And true to his word, the leader now had three fearful dragons in his possession. Two other adults each had a young one in tow.

The leader pointed to the last youngster—the one with the torn wing. He came forward to recite his riddle.

CHAPTER 31

Duck warned me.

Gwendolyn squirmed as she tried to settle down for the night. It was normal to feel a little uneasy during a full moon, but she couldn't remember ever feeling overwhelming anxiety for no good reason. Something felt terribly wrong, but what?

Earlier in the day Ruthe came with the bucket, twirled around and sang a rollicking tune about the Harvest Festival with its bonfires, dancing, trading, and gossip.

That's it! Gwendolyn thought with relief. *The humans' festival is coming. Maybe the farmer will take some of the piglets.*

As a young pig, Gwendolyn was taken from her family to the gathering of the humans. A stranger argued with her first human over the pig.

"She's a beautiful pig—best of the litter," her first human said. "She'll bear many piglets. But I'll let you have her for less than she's worth."

To her surprise, the second man scoffed, "The best of the litter? Well, I shouldn't like to see the others then, if your best is so scrawny. To sell her for less than she's worth, you'll have to give her away. I'll take her off your hands for three silver coins."

"Three? Seven is more like it and still a bargain."

"Don't be daft, man. I'll be lucky if she lives until I get her home."

And so it had gone. The pig hated to leave the human who obviously valued her to go with one who thought her worthless. Gwendolyn smiled as she remembered her astonishment when the farmer told Ruthe he'd gotten a perfect pig for a good price.

Duck warned me. Some of the piglets will probably go live on different farms. That must be the reason I'm feeling so unsettled. I'll miss the piglets as much as Strange One, but I'll know what kind of predictable life they'll have. I won't have to worry about them as much as I do him.

Then Gwendolyn remembered—tonight's full moon followed the equal day and night. *Is Strange One at the dragon gathering? Is he safe? Could my anxiety be some sort of premonition?*

CHAPTER 32

What other naming powers are you withholding?

Is this the dragon Mama saw? What's the penalty for a wrong guess? Strange One's heart beat faster and almost drowned out the riddle.

The young dragon with the torn wing spoke fearfully. "Destruction and ruin a dragon's delight; It follows the path of my terrible flight."

The leader looked around the circle to see if anyone ventured to guess.

Strange One, still uncertain if he dared to answer, eased from the shadows of the trees. *The riddle fits the name. I can't help it if Mama told me his name. I could have guessed it myself,* Strange One rationalized as he tried to convince himself he was being fair. *And I'm not trying to get a servant. Maybe he can be a friend.* He moved through the rows of dragons and left his silence.

"Rek," Strange One announced. *What is the penalty for a wrong guess?* "His name is Rek."

Rek looked flabbergasted, and the she-dragon snapped, "I knew you would be the one to lose." She hung her head in humiliation.

The leader spoke to Strange One, "It is obvious that you have guessed correctly. You now have a servant until the next gathering—unusual for one your age. Your coloring announces that this is your first gathering also. Odd that you did not come forward before. What is your naming riddle?"

Strange One now knew the price for speaking—the risk of losing his own freedom. But he had prepared while standing in the shadows. He took a deep breath.

"Raised by one of black and white,
And taught by feathered wing,
Dragon's egg, but not her child
Though dragon just the same."

Strange One's heart pounded at the sight of the leader's frown. *He really, really wants to own me. Don't guess. Don't guess.* Strange One watched the leader's glance sweep the gathered dragons inviting another to name and humble this cocky youngster.

No one stood forward to hazard a guess.

"Take your prize," the leader growled.

Rek looked to his mother, who clamped her jaws and merged into the crowd. He hung his head and moved beside Strange One.

"Let the dragon games begin," bellowed the leader.

"Now to fight, fly, flame. Now to win, win, win!" the gathering answered.

"What happens now?" Strange One asked Rek as the throng milled around them and reformed into smaller groups.

"Don't you know?"

Strange One shook his head.

"We divide by age to have contests," answered Rek.

"What kind of contests?"

"All kinds—like hunting, flying, flaming, riddling, storytelling. Come on, it looks like flying will be first. The winner in our group gets gold to start his treasure."

As they got into position, Strange One noticed that both males and females raced.

As all the youngsters jostled for position, they called insults to each other.

"I've seen you fly. You couldn't win a race with a crow!"

Someone shoved Rek, "Lame-brained and wing-scarred, you haven't got a chance."

Table Scraps and I tease each other, but not like the dragons do. They're trying to be mean.

Rek whispered, "He's right. I don't have a chance with a torn wing. Do you think you do?"

"I don't know. Why?"

"Don't you know anything except my name? I want you to win so there will be less shame in being in service to you. I'll block for you if I can."

"Quiet!" the leader commanded. "You will circle that peak and return. The winner will receive this golden medallion from my own treasure. Prepare! Fly!"

The start was a confusion of thrashing wings and nipping teeth. Sharp claws scratched Strange One's thigh. Finally, the dragons took off and spread apart. Strange One lowered his head and looked straight at the peak. He pumped his wings as his head led like a needle poking a hole in the air currents.

Bit by bit, Strange One gained on the dragons in the lead. He dipped one wing and curved around the peak. He passed one dragon. Only two others remained in front.

He pulled alongside the second place dragon, who arched his neck to raise his head. Strange One passed as the dragon slowed and lunged.

The other dragon's teeth didn't penetrate muscle, but did scrape furrows in Strange One's leg.

Strange One yelped in pain and tried to pull his own head up to defend himself. He wobbled, then lowered his head again and raced out of the dragon's reach.

He couldn't catch the front-runner who landed moments ahead of him.

The leader tossed the medallion to the winner, but his eyes were on Strange One. "You don't fly like a dragon," he said. Then, to the whole gathering, he announced, "It is time to feast! Hunters, show us your skill."

Young dragons, including Rek, again took to the sky. But Strange One faded into the crowd. He found a group of adults who vied to out-do each other with stories.

When Strange One listened to Ruthe's stories, all the dragons were evil villains. Strange One longed for new tales. *We'll be the heroes in our own stories.*

The dragons in these stories were heroes only in name—they did the same things as the dragons in Ruthe's stories. But the tellers of these tales praised and celebrated the dragons who pillaged whole towns for treasure they would never spend and who disdained weakness even in their own young. *These stories are worse than Ruthe's. I want heroes that do good things.*

The hunters returned with prey. Dragons flamed and cooked their catch. The aroma of sizzling meat filled the air and tantalized Strange One. But the sight of frenzied eating revolted him.

The carnivores greedily bit and pulled at whatever had been flamed. They ripped animals apart and tore food away from each other.

Strange One looked closer. The largest of the hunted animals were deer and cattle. Strange One thought of the patient cows he'd known on the farm. He stepped back.

"Why aren't you feasting?" The leader's question was a veiled accusation.

"I'm not hungry."

The enormous dragon laughed. "What does hunger have to do with it? Have your servant bring some proper food."

Rek quickly approached with the hind quarter of a sheep.

"Eat," commanded the leader. Other dragons stopped gobbling to watch the confrontation.

"Flame it and eat it," Rek quietly urged. "I don't want to be in service to an outcast. Do what the leader told you."

Strange One bent his head over the sheep's body. *I can't eat a farm animal even if I could flame it. And it's wrong to kill any animal when I'm not even hungry.* He shook his head, and raised up.

"You reject the ways of dragons?" A white-hot flame from the leader scorched Strange One's muzzle.

"Flame back," Rek coached.

Strange One shifted his eyes to Rek and whispered, "I can't."

In that instant, the leader dipped his head and came up under Strange One's unprotected chest. Sharp teeth penetrated the young dragon's scales and muscles.

Strange One sucked back a cry. *I can't let him know how much he hurt me.* His heart beat wildly. *Just let go. I'll fly away and you'll never see me again.*

But the red dragon held fast.

The pain surged, then ebbed into numbness. At last, Strange One heard Rek's frantic hissing.

"Riddles—fight with riddles."

Riddles. Think, think. How should I challenge him?

Strange One wheezed:

"Riddles my weapons.

Answers my shield.

Though you battle with wit,

I'll never yield."

The teeth released Strange One's chest. The other dragons sighed collectively in disappointment. But the confrontation was not over.

"My wit is sharp," responded the leader, "as sharp as my claws and teeth. One wound means your life as surely as this battle will."

"And if my riddle wounds you?" asked Strange One.

"You and your servant leave here alive. You, as an unnatural dragon, are outcast and banished from the gatherings forever. This poor fool," he indicated Rek, "has the misfortune to be in-service to you until the next gathering, when he may return . . . if, of course, he dares, since we all know Rek's name."

The crowd laughed.

The leader continued, "You chose the weapons of riddles. Therefore, I begin the duel.

"Treasure is our pleasure,
Gold is our joy.
From whom is it better—
Baby, man, or boy?"

Strange One tried to remember Ruthe's every story and the pig's every riddle. He ignored the pain of his wound as he searched for the one piece he could use to begin to construct the puzzle.

"You must answer, fool," prodded the leader whose red scales were now glowing with the excitement of battle and victory.

"None of those, and yet all," ventured Strange One. "The finest gold comes from the dwarves who have the faces of old men, the height of boys, and the temper tantrums of babies."

The red dragon's glow faded, and Strange One tried to remember one of Gwendolyn's riddles. He recited the first one she taught him.

"After the rain and before the dance, I grow in a circle ever wider. What am I?"

The dragons all groaned and the leader smiled, "What do you take me for—a simpleton? Even the youngest dragon knows that is a fairy ring.

"Now, I will tell you the name riddle I told at my first gathering. Do what no dragon has done and guess my name, if you can."

Strange One's heart sank, and his wounded chest throbbed.

Surely I'll die before the sun rises.

"Wait!" the large blue dragon shouted from the crowd. "You cannot offer your naming-riddle when you have not guessed his, which was given first. You forfeit your turn."

The crowd nodded agreement, and the leader glowered. Not only had he lost a turn in the duel, but the challenge on the part of the blue signaled a threat to his leadership.

Strange One had one more chance. What if all the riddles from Gwendolyn were too easy? But she had told him one thing male dragons didn't know. He strained to make his knowledge fit the riddle pattern.

"Dragon heat and dragon flame,
From whence they come?
Give the name."

The leader looked baffled. Hesitantly, he answered, "We don't know exactly how we get fire. Some have noticed they have fire after eating bachelor's buttons. So that's my answer. Bachelor's buttons."

"Wrong name and wrong answer.
The she-dragons will know I speak true
When I answer feverfew."

There was a sharp intake of breath by the females. "How did he know?" asked one.

The others shushed her. Strange One strained to hear, hoping one of them would slip with whatever else was needed for fire. But the females were trying to calm the males even as they shrank from flaming anger.

"He's wrong! bachelor's buttons are just bachelor's buttons."

"There is no weed called feverfew. That dragon is just making things up."

The leader roared, "What other naming powers are you withholding?"

"None. We're not withholding anything. The strange dragon

doesn't know anything. He doesn't even have fire himself. It's not true!"

"He said 'feverfew,' and you gave yourselves away, you traitors to the power of the leader. We know he is right. What other secrets are you keeping?"

During the bitter argument, Strange One slipped away and flew to his cave.

Rek followed.

CHAPTER 33

Maybe I should have taught him to fight.

Something's happened to Strange One. Did he go to the gathering? I saw how vicious dragons are. Maybe I should have taught him to fight. Is he even alive?

Gwendolyn tried not to think of other possibilities. Had he reverted to typical dragon behavior? Was Strange One now the danger she feared when he first hatched?

Gwendolyn pictured Strange One with beastly, wolf-like eyes— a hunter who knew exactly where to find farm animals, including seven nearly-mature piglets.

Gwendolyn shook herself. *Maybe I'm just dreading the upcoming Harvest Festival or winter; maybe I'm just over-tired; maybe . . .*

Chapter 34

You don't know the first thing about acting like a proper dragon.

"What?" Strange One gasped after the struggle to fly back to the cave. Each pump of his wings pulled the edges of the chest wounds apart.

"I said, where do I sleep?" Rek asked again.

"Here, of course."

"But this is your hall. And these side tunnels are only big enough for something the size of a sheep. So where do I sleep?"

"Here," Strange managed to whisper.

"Here? Together? Oh, no. Dragons do not live together. When dragons are young or in-service, they live in a cave with mother or master, but . . ." Rek's voice rose in irritation, "even then they have a separate tunnel. We . . . never . . . share."

Rek eyed the cave again. "Where's your treasure?"

"Don't have any," Strange One's voice weakened further.

"I'm in service to a dragon who has less treasure than I do?" Rek asked. "And there isn't even a place for me to sleep in this miserable cave." He brightened as a sparkle caught his eye. "But a crystal is a sign of power. Your powers are unusual. How did you know about . . . what's the other name for bachelor's button?"

"Feverfew," Strange One croaked. *Should I answer the question about how I know? Will Rek use knowledge against me? I must sound like a master. My chest hurts. Can't hold head up. Too hard to think.* "It's time to sleep, and both of us sleep in this chamber."

Rek frowned but moved to obey. He lay as far from Strange One's sleeping spot as he could get.

Strange One slept fitfully. The puncture wounds were hot and inflamed. He floated in and out of sleep. Dreams, memories, and reality joined in one stream. At times, Strange One lifted a heavy eyelid and saw no one. At other times, he dreamed he shared his cave with another creature.

Finally, his body cooled. He drifted between moments of wakefulness and healthful sleep. He heard a voice that soothed like the lapping of water,

"What's your name? What's your name?"

"Str . . ." he began, then caught himself. His eyes flew open. Rek sat beside him. Memories of the gathering returned.

"I'm thirsty," Strange One rasped. "Bring me a branch dipped in the lake so I can lick the water from the leaves."

Rek obeyed without a word and made several trips before Strange One's thirst was quenched.

After Rek's last trip, Strange One asked, "You stayed. Tell me why." *Did Rek stay out of duty? Was he worried about me or does he want company too?*

Rek said nothing.

"Why did you stay?"

After another moment of hesitation, Rek answered, "If you told me your name, I could take your naming riddle to the next gathering. I could claim the secret and power of your name. The name Rek would be forgotten. But now . . ." Rek hung his head.

"Oh." Strange One also hung his head in disappointment. "Is that why you saved me at the gathering when you told me to fight with riddles, so you could try to claim my name?"

"No, I hadn't thought of it then. If the leader had defeated you, I would have been in-service to him for a year. Who would you rather serve?" Rek asked.

"I see what you mean." Strange One smiled.

Rek startled, then grinned back. "It's better to serve a master who isn't too dragon-like, and you don't know the first thing about acting like a proper dragon."

"Yes, I do. Bring me food."

"I know a close-by farm. I'll get a goat."

"No goat!" Strange One paused for a moment. *I can't say I don't want to eat farm animals. How can I say it in a way that sounds like a dragon?* He lowered his voice and stated, "I eat nothing tamed. Tame prey is only for weaklings or lazy hunters."

Rek left the cave with a shrug.

I don't think I sounded tough enough, but I figured something out. I won't eat any animal that hasn't been taught how to protect itself—so no farm animals. I will hunt creatures who are part of the wild give and take. But I won't hunt more than I need. He remembered the fox the farmer gave him. *And I'll try not to hunt animals with young. I already promised not to hunt birds or the animals around the cave. And a promise is a promise.*

Strange One felt a deep comfort in finding his own way.

I'll have Rek for company now. So even though I will never, ever go to a dragon gathering again, and even though I got hurt, I'm glad I went one time. And maybe Rek and I will become friends before a year is over.

Strange One smiled in satisfaction and ate the two squirrels Rek brought back.

※※※

One evening, after his wounds healed, the two dragons walked through a meadow, and Strange One asked, "Do you know Hog the Rock?"

"No, is it like Hoard the Crown?"

With a mischievous grin, Strange One dropped a toad-sized rock between his forepaws. "Get it if you can," he called.

Rek made a half-hearted move for the rock and pulled back. "Guess you're just better at this than I am," he said, then turned to continue their walk to the lake.

"Rek, wait. I want to play."

Rek turned back and made another lunge for the rock. He purposely missed.

"What's wrong with you, Rek? Don't you want to have fun?" Strange One waited for an answer, but Rek stayed silent. "Well, don't you?" Strange One pushed.

"Master, you said you wanted to play. I obeyed. What a servant wants isn't important."

"What do **you** want, Rek?"

"I want treasure. I want the year to be over. I don't want to get bitten and ripped."

"I can't promise you treasure, but I won't hurt you. I don't want a servant. I want a friend."

"Dragons don't have friends. You don't know how to be a dragon."

"But we could be friends. We only bite the rock in Hog the Rock. We don't bite each other."

"Just the rock? Maybe it's not like Hoard the Crown. I'll try," Rek agreed.

Strange One stood over the rock and Rek darted. Strange One scooped up the rock and danced backwards. But Rek was fast and grabbed the rock on his next try.

Soon the two dragons forgot about the rock. They pounced and rolled, chased and tumbled. Although they mouthed and held each other with teeth, neither bore down. Neither punctured a scale on the other nor tore at the other's leathery wings.

As they romped, Rek grew less guarded and more playful. Finally, they rolled apart and lay panting like two puppies.

"So what else do friends do?" asked Rek.

"Share and look out for each other."

"So, since you know my name, you'll tell me yours, right . . . friend?"

Strange One stayed silent.

"I thought so, Master. Now what?"

"Let's tell stories. I mean, would you like to tell stories?

"Only if you go first."

Strange One told a story he had always hoped to hear about a dragon who rescued a princess.

Rek looked puzzled. "The dragon didn't eat the princess?"

Strange One shook his head. *Rek missed the point.* "They became friends. Of course, he didn't eat her."

Then Rek told a story of a dragon who flamed villages. When the humans fled, he took everything precious. Soon his cave was nearly filled with coins and jewelry. But the dragon wasn't happy, because the villagers weren't rich.

"Why did he want all those things?" Strange One interrupted. "Why did he keep wanting more?"

"Well, why wouldn't he?" Rek retorted. "He might get to be a powerful leader. He could fight knights. All other creatures would be afraid of him."

"Is that what you want, Rek?"

"That's what all dragons want. Don't you? Why are you so strange, anyway? You don't know anything about dragons except my name and about eating feverfew. How did you know that?"

"My mama taught me, but she didn't know the rest of how to get fire. Do you know?"

"No. I had to eat bach . . . feverfew twice. Mother made fun of me and told me to remember the names she called me when I ate it again. I still get angry when I think of it." Smoke curled from the corners of Rek's mouth.

"But at least she taught us how to fight and take care of ourselves. Who ever heard of a mother who doesn't teach her children how to fight or flame?" Rek shook his head in disbelief. "What kind of a dragon is she?"

What should I tell a servant? What would I tell a friend? Strange One made his decision.

"She's not exactly a dragon. Rek, I was raised by a pig who found my egg. A duck taught me to fly with my head held low so I can go faster. A human told us stories about dragons."

Rek's eyes widened, and his mouth dropped open. In a hoarse whisper, he said, "No wonder you aren't like other dragons. How did you know about the gathering?"

"The same way I knew your name. My mama hid in a dragon's cave, your mother's cave, and heard secrets."

Strange One waited for Rek's anger to flare, but instead the little dragon laughed.

"What a tale I will have to tell when I am no longer in-service to you. And won't the joke be on my mother when the next gathering finds out how a he-dragon learned the secret of feverfew and how she was tricked by a pig!"

"Rek, when I guessed your name, I wanted a friend, not a servant. You can't be both. You are released from service."

"You mean, I can go anywhere and do anything I want? What if you change your mind?"

"I give up all power to command you . . . ever. I can't take back knowing your name, but I can make us equal. My name is Strange One."

Will Rek stay now—as my friend? Strange One held his breath.

Rek gazed into Strange One's eyes, then left without another word.

Nothing's changed. I don't belong with pigs or dragons. Strange One choked back a sob. *I don't belong anywhere.*

CHAPTER 35

Most of the piglets were crying.

Gwendolyn dug furiously. *How could I be so blind? The humans take the hens' eggs and sometimes even eat the chickens. Why did I think the humans know that pigs are different? I should have fought when the farmer shooed me into the stable by myself and boarded the opening.*

I heard everything the farmer and that woman said as they captured each of the piglets and tethered them to stakes.

❋ ❋ ❋

"When we sell them, we will have the money for our taxes and perhaps enough for the tools we need," the farmer said. "Next year we should be able to keep one or two from the sow's litter."

The woman asked, "Do you think they will all fetch good prices, Husband?"

The farmer checked the stakes and the knots holding the piglets as he spoke. "The big male will. He'll make a fine breeder, I wager. We can only hope next year's litter produces one so fine. And the biggest female is also likely to be a brooder. Who knows about the rest? But probably they will make fine feasts for the townsfolk."

Gwendolyn stood frozen in shock. *My children eaten!*

The woman spoke, "It saddens me to think of Gwendolyn's children butchered."

Ruthe saved Strange One's life. She'll save the piglets too.

The pig trembled as she listened for the rest of the conversation.

"Ruthe," the farmer reminded, "this is the way of farm life, which is the reason you never should have named that pig. For now you think of these porkers as someone's children."

"I know, but I'm still sad it has to be that way," Ruthe answered.

That woman isn't even arguing for the lives of my children!

The farmer checked the boards that trapped Gwendolyn in the stable. "Your Gwendolyn will be safe in here until we return. The other pigs are ready to travel tomorrow morning. It will be a fine festival this year."

The humans walked to their cottage.

※ ※ ※

Gwendolyn flung herself against the immovable boards. "I will not let them be taken away to be slain!" She searched for another exit and found none.

She peered between the boards. Most of the piglets were crying—Buttercup most of all, although she, as the largest female, would most likely go to another farm. Gwendolyn ached as she watched Nasturtium comfort Buttercup. Nasturtium, strong, wise Nasturtium who, as the runt, would most certainly be killed for what food she could provide.

This is wrong! Gwendolyn began digging in a frenzy. But the pigs themselves had packed the soil so tightly that digging a tunnel was hopeless. *Even if I can dig out of the stable in time, how will I get them untied? And then would we have time to dig out of the pen?*

How can I save my children? They can't fly away like Strange One did. Gwendolyn sank to the ground in misery and listened to the frightened wailing of the piglets.

"Pig, are you in there?" Duck demanded. "What's going on?"

Maybe there's hope.

CHAPTER 36

Are you crazy?

Of course Rek wanted to leave. *I left the farm because I wanted to choose for myself. But I'm not sorry I claimed him. We played. We know each other's names. We're equal.*

Strange One looked at the dusky sky, hoping to see Rek—hoping his worries weren't real. *Rek knows my name and where my cave is. I only know his name. He has fire, but I don't. Maybe we're not really equal. Is Rek more dragon or more friend?*

If Rek didn't come soon, Strange One would leave to hunt by himself another night. He saw a dot on the horizon. As the dot grew closer, it elongated. Strange One could see that it flew with its head down and straight. *Maybe Rek is flying like a duck is get here faster. I hope . . . no, there's no dragon tail.*

He slumped and turned to walk in the direction of the nearby lake. He had gone only a few heavy steps when a harsh voice made him jump.

"Turning your back on an old friend now, are you? Your mother would be ashamed."

"Duck!" Strange One whipped around. "Duck, is it really you?"

"Of course it's me. What other bird would fly right up and say hello to a dragon? A dragon with no manners, I might add."

"Is Mama all right? How are the piglets? I bet Table Scraps is as big as Mama, isn't he? Duck, how did you find me?"

"You never could ask just one question at a time like a sensible animal. For a flying creature, finding a dragon isn't hard. Usually you just look for a scorched hillside. But this time I had to use more brains, so I asked other birds if they knew of a dragon with no fire. You are still fireless?"

Strange One nodded glumly.

"Well, I did my part. You can still fly, right?"

"Of course!"

"Good, because the pig sent me to fetch you. The piglets are in danger."

"What kind of danger?"

"The humans are taking them to some kind of gathering where they will be sold. At first your mother was sad, but not worried. But then she heard the farmer say that some of the piglets would be used for food."

Icy fear gripped Strange One.

"Pig sent me," Duck continued, "to fetch you to save them. So we best be going now."

A sudden gust of wind rustled the tree tops. Strange One glanced up, then hissed, "Quickly, into the cave! Hide in one of the small tunnels."

Duck needed no further urging. She ran, flapping her wings, into the darkness.

Strange One watched the dragon prepare to land, and he whispered, "Why now, Rek? Do you come in friendship—friendship that will include my family?"

Rek landed and grinned. Finally, he simply said, "I missed you."

"I missed you too, Rek."

"Strange One," Rek seemed to struggle with the unfamiliarity of using of a name, "Are you hungry? We could go hunting?"

"I can't."

"Well, would you like to play Hog the Rock or tell stories?"

"I can't tonight."

"Oh." Rek grappled for his next words. "I liked what you said about wanting a friend . . ." he waited a moment.

When Strange One made no response, Rek covered his embarrassment, "Well, at least I can see the crystal before I go."

He entered the cave before Strange One could stop him. Rek chattered on, "My cave has two entrances and plenty of room for treasure. Someday I'll have lots. I don't have a crystal though."

Rek looked all around the main chamber. "It's just like I remembered it. I really liked the stories you used to tell." He glanced hopefully at Strange One. When Strange One still didn't answer, Rek hung his head. "You want me to leave, don't you?"

"Not really," Strange One murmured.

"Yes," quacked Duck.

"What was that?"

Strange One shook his head.

"He already told you he can't do anything with you now, so just go away."

Rek sniffed at each of the tunnels. "You've got fowl in here, Strange One. What's happening?"

"My family is in danger, and I have to help them."

"So you can just leave now," snapped Duck from the safety of the narrow tunnel.

Rek ignored her. "Are you going to rescue them just like in a story?"

"Yes," answered Strange One.

"Can I help?"

"No!" shouted Duck.

Strange One vacillated. *How much has Rek changed? Will he think of pigs and ducks as food? He does still want to fill his cave with treasure.*

From the tunnel, Duck argued, "Send that over-grown lizard away. You can never really trust a dragon."

"What do you think I am?" Strange One reacted. He turned to Rek. "Will you be brave and true?"

Rek nodded.

Duck muttered, "He's as stubborn as the pig." She waddled out of the tunnel and looked at Strange One. "Once this dragon eats me, you'll know you can't trust him with your brothers and sisters."

Duck and Rek glared at each other. Strange One glanced from one to the other, feeling helpless to resolve their mistrust.

"And just what can a duck do to rescue Strange One's family?" Rek asked.

"I've done plenty!" retorted Duck.

"Like what?"

"Like finding..."

"Stop!" interjected Strange One. "This fighting isn't helping the piglets. Rek, Duck has shown she is brave and true. Duck, think of how much two dragons can do."

"I'm ready," affirmed Rek.

"Are you crazy?" Duck squawked. "I know what dragons can do!"

Chapter 37

Humans seemed even more dangerous than dragons.

Nothing in the quiet farmyard muffled the memory of the piglets' final cries of distress. Gwendolyn felt those sounds would echo in her mind for the rest of her life. *Did Duck find Strange One? Where are they? Have the piglets and the humans reached the gathering yet?*

Not only had her world shrunk to this lonely stable; it had turned upside down—for now the humans seemed even more dangerous than dragons.

Gwendolyn remembered how fears squeezed her throat when the wolf chased her and when she was hiding in the dragon cave. Now the terror of knowing danger encircled her children and that she could do nothing choked her even more tightly.

She continued to flail at the slight indentation she'd dug in the packed soil. She had to do something.

CHAPTER 38

I knew you had to want treasure.

Strange One, Rek, and Duck formed an unbalanced triangle as each looked from one to the other.

Strange One's thoughts raced. *Should Rek come or not? Is it possible humans own other dragons that I might have to fight?* He flinched with the memory of his past wounds.

"If we have to fight," he said aloud, "is it better to have a duck with me or a fire-breathing dragon?"

Rek tried to stifle a laugh.

Duck's expression blazed with anger.

"But," Strange One continued, "I know Duck will do anything to save the piglets. Rek is untried."

"I want to be tried. I want to be a hero." The plea in Rek's eyes seemed sincere to Strange One. "Trust me to do this and help your family."

"Hah!" snorted Duck. "Trust a dragon!"

Again her words pushed Strange One. "You trust me, Duck. And I trust Rek. All three of us will fly toward the road and follow it. When we reach the humans' gathering, Rek and I will shield the piglets from the humans. Duck, you'll fly low to lead the piglets back here. When you get far enough away from the humans, Rek and I will catch up with you."

"That sounds exciting . . . and easy," said Rek.

Duck muttered, "Easy to feast on piglets then."

Strange One ignored her. "Maybe," he said to Rek. "But we don't know for sure how far away their festival is, or how many humans will be there, or what kind of weapons they have. Let's fly!"

Duck faced Rek, "You go first, lizard. I don't want you to forget yourself and gobble me because there's food in front of your face."

Rek led the procession out of the cave where the three took off and flew in silence as the moon arced through the sky. Once they landed to drink from a lake.

Duck spoke to Rek, "I see that dragons fly like ducks."

"Not really," answered Rek. "We usually fly so we're ready to attack. But Strange One taught me to fly his way. It's faster."

"I taught him everything he knows about flying!" Duck swaggered up the bank.

Again they flew following the moon-lit ribbon of packed soil that marked the humans' road. They flew with heads held out straight and low, wings rhythmically pumping. They flew until the sky lightened to gray and the earliest birds twittered.

They found the gathering in a large meadow where a second road intersected the road they followed. Make-shift tents ringed a large open area. Loaded wagons and livestock surrounded the ring of tents.

The three circled. A horse neighed, and the camp began to waken. Strange One was the first to spot the piglets who were tethered to a single pole near a cluster of tents. He motioned Rek to stay behind on the road. Strange One and Duck swooped to the ground.

Everything happened at once.

Table Scraps squealed, "He's come! Strange One came to rescue us!"

Duck tried to hush the piglet, but the others jumped to their feet. They squealed, squirmed, and further tangled their ropes. Ruthe and the farmer rushed out of the nearest tent.

"It's Gwendolyn's dragon!" Ruthe slowed, but continued to move toward Strange One and the piglets. She held out her hand. "You remember me, don't you?" she said soothingly.

The farmer pushed ahead. "Stay away from my pigs!" He waved a stick in Strange One's face.

More humans emerged from the other tents. Men with heavy staves maneuvered to surround the dragon and the piglets. One with a bow stopped to pull an arrow from his quiver. Another hefted a spear. To Strange One, the tips of the arrow and the spear looked like sharp teeth, and he caught his breath.

"Help us, Strange One!" wailed Buttercup.

The dragon looked at his brothers and sisters, each tied around the neck, each trying to pull free. Even Table Scraps had terror in his eyes.

Pure rage, beyond any anger he had ever known, flamed in Strange One's chest. *How dare the humans do this to my brothers and sisters?* The dragon's eyes shone like embers. The heat in his chest spread up his throat and singed the roof of his mouth. Strange One faced the farmer and spread his mouth wide to roar his fury.

Like an explosion, flames leapt from his jaws with his bellow of indignation.

The farmer froze in surprise and horror. Other humans retreated. The archer let his arrow fly.

It struck Strange One's scar where the leader's teeth had ripped away protective scales.

The pain shot deep. Strange One caught his breath and closed his eyes. When he opened them again, he saw the man with the spear taking aim. Strange One fought the urge to flee. He heard Nasturtium's cry. That sound of her fear hurt more deeply than any pain from teeth, arrows, or spears. He stood firm and focused on the stake that held the piglets' bonds.

Knives of flame cut the ropes as the piglets strained to get away from the heat. The spear went high and bounced off one of the plates along Strange One's backbone.

At the snap of the ropes, Strange One shouted, "Duck, lead them back down the road past Rek. He and I will keep the humans from the chase. Piglets, follow! Run! Table Scraps, go!"

Duck flew low guiding the racing piglets. She didn't slow as she passed Rek, who blocked the humans. Strange One roared when another arrow grazed his shoulder. Smoke and flames licked the air.

The farmer moved in front of Ruthe to protect her. Strange One noticed his beard and one eyebrow had been singed. He looked at the two humans and felt a deep ache. The dragon's anger cooled.

"I do not wish to hurt you," he said in words he knew the humans couldn't understand. "You didn't kill me when I was small and weak. And now, you are protecting Ruthe, your real treasure. But I must protect mine."

Once more, fire flickered as Strange One roared, "Do not try to reclaim the piglets!"

The flames did not reach as far as they had before.

Strange One flew to Rek's side. Together the dragons roared and flamed as other men approached. Hands moved to cover faces or to protect leather pouches. Strange One glanced at Rek whose eyes gleamed as he focused on the money bags.

"Gold coins," Rek murmured. "Treasure." His tongue flickered greedily, and he stepped towards a man with a bulging pouch.

Several humans slipped past the distracted dragon and ran down the road following the piglets.

Strange One whipped his head from the side of the road he was guarding. "Rek!"

But Rek took another step closer to the man. With fumbling

hands, the man untied the pouch from his waist and tossed it to the ground.

Strange One could not block the swarm of humans by himself, and the piglets were not yet far enough away. "Rek!"

But Rek was no longer in service; he need not obey. Rek bent and picked up the pouch in his mouth.

"Rek!" Strange One begged in desperation as another man circled past him. "Please save my treasure!"

Finally, Rek looked at Strange One and the road. The men who had slipped by had almost reached the panicked piglets. Onion's squeal seemed to break Rek's spell. He flew in pursuit.

Duck quacked frantically as a man jumped at Buttercup and grabbed her hind leg.

Rek roared. His flames incinerated the pouch he carried in his jaws. Silver and gold coins flew to the ground, but Rek seemed not to notice, and the man released Buttercup. The humans scattered.

Rek hovered protectively at the rear of the piglets while Duck led them further down the road.

Strange One continued to block. His roars and flames kept the rest of the humans at bay. He glanced over his shoulder to see Rek's form flying over a cloud of dust. Another arrow struck Strange One's neck. He winced, but it didn't go deep. He knocked it away.

Strange One looked back again. The dust was settling—a sign the piglets had left the road and turned into the forest. In moments, they would be safe from the humans.

Then Strange One looked into Ruthe's anguished eyes. *She understands.* He roared at the humans once more, but there was no flame. *She will tell different stories now—stories with dragon heroes. But I'll never hear them. We, the farmer, Ruthe, and I are much alike. But we'll never share lives again. This fight is over.*

Strange One took to the sky. Soon he caught up with Rek. They flew at a pig's pace over the forest. Down below, Strange One could see that Duck and all the piglets were safe, whole, and free.

Rek smiled. "I knew you had to . . ." he made a funny face. "I've got something in my mouth." He shifted his jaws around. "I think it's one of the gold pieces. Anyway, I knew you had to want treasure. I just didn't know it could be something better than gold."

Better than gold! Does Rek truly understand? Can he be trusted on his own? Strange One had one more piece of treasure to collect. *Do I dare risk the piglets? Will that be too much temptation for Rek?*

Rek chattered on, "When you claimed me with my name, I lost dragon power. I wanted to get it back with gold and treasure. You have a different kind of power. I don't understand it yet. But maybe I can have that kind of power too," he ended wistfully.

Strange One dared. "Rek," he said, "will you take the piglets to the cave and guard them from the forest's dangers?"

Rek glowed with pride. "Yes!"

"And can I have your gold piece?"

Rek looked doubtful, but after a moment, he spit it to Strange One and asked, "Where are you going?"

CHAPTER 39

She could not calm her fear.

Gwendolyn tried to focus on farm wisdom—the wisdom found in patient waiting. *Seeds planted too soon rot. Fruit eaten too early tastes tart. I have to be patient. Don't the humans say "no news is good news."* But she could not calm her fear.

"If I can just know they've escaped and are alive and safe, I will never ask for anything again—ever! Duck, hurry back. Where are my children?"

A hen peered through a space between the boards and looked at the pig with pity. She clucked sympathetically, "It's hard, dearie, but you'll get used to it. There will be more babies next year."

"I won't get used to it!" The infuriated pig charged the boards with a roar. The hen flapped her wings and squawked in her rush to get away. Gwendolyn fell backwards in a daze.

"There's an easier way out. Stand back."

The pig looked up and saw a yellow eye looking down at her through a high crack. "Strange One!" She sprang to her feet. "Are the piglets safe?"

"Yes, Mama. Duck is leading them to my cave. Now stand as far back as you can."

Gwendolyn hugged the back wall. Strange One opened his mouth. Flames erupted and burned two boards. Strange One stomped out the flames and broke away the boards. Gwendolyn rushed out of the stable.

"Fire! How . . ."

Strange One flew to perch on the fence's top rail. The weight of his full-grown body crashed through the top, middle and bottom rails forming three V's. Gwendolyn pranced over the broken fence. She trotted to the road, but stopped when she noticed Strange One walking to the cottage. As she looked over her shoulder, she saw the dragon spit out a golden disc, which landed in front of the door.

"Let's go!" he shouted and flew to catch up with the pig.

Once they left the road, passed through woods, and reached a clearing, Strange One landed and walked with Gwendolyn. They talked about the rescue, their time apart, and Rek.

Gwendolyn fretted, "This dragon, Rek, are you sure he can be trusted?"

"Mama, you sound like Duck. Yes, or I wouldn't have left my treasure with him."

Is it possible that other dragons can be good like Strange One? Gwendolyn wondered.

When the forest was thick without enough space for Strange One to fit between tree trunks, he flew above her until the next clearing gave him room to land again.

"Mama, for a long time after the dragon gathering and after Rek left, I felt as though I was neither pig nor dragon.

"You taught me to hide my anger so I wouldn't hurt anyone, but dragon fire only comes with anger. I had to feel it so I could save the piglets. Because I wasn't raised by dragons, the anger doesn't fill my whole life, and the fire is contained. I can decide when to use it.

"And now, instead of feeling as though I don't belong anywhere, I know that I'm both pig and dragon. My place is sometimes lonely, but I'm connected to two worlds."

Gwendolyn pondered his words as they walked in silent companionship.

Finally, Strange One announced, "This is my home."

Gwendolyn hurried into the cave. She squinted to see in the dim light. There were no sounds other than the soft snores of a sleeping dragon.

"Piglets!" she called in alarm.

"Mama's here!" Onion squealed as she rushed from one of the side tunnels.

The sleeping dragon opened first one then the second eyelid.

Sweet Pea, Truffle, and Nasturtium followed Onion and gathered around Gwendolyn. Buttercup peeked out from the middle tunnel. Table Scraps and Seven galloped from the last tunnel just as Strange One reached the room.

Gwendolyn nuzzled each piglet. Then she gazed at the dragon who watched quietly. She walked over to him.

"You must be Rek. I have much to thank you for."

The red spot on his forehead brightened and spread, then flared once again when Gwendolyn nuzzled him in the same manner she had greeted the piglets.

"Well," harrumphed Duck as she finally emerged from the middle tunnel. "And I suppose it's too much to expect that I'll be thanked for rescuing the piglets and keeping them from ending as dragon dinner!" She glared at Rek.

He glared back.

Table Scraps jumped to the dragon's defense, "Rek wouldn't try to eat us."

"Only because I watched him like a hawk every minute," retorted Duck.

"That's right," confirmed Buttercup. "Duck didn't sleep at all."

"Like she could do anything if . . ." Rek trailed off, then whispered to himself, "I won't get mad."

"Well, Rek didn't try to take one nibble. I bet dragons don't even eat pigs anyway," Seven glowered at Buttercup.

Even Rek looked surprised, "No, Seven, you have to be careful of dragons. They're not like Strange One and me . . ."

"Not yet!" Strange One added.

Duck rolled her eyes.

Gwendolyn smiled at the familiar pandemonium. She thought nothing could ever cause her grief again.

Chapter 40

I'm glad you were the one who found my egg.

Strange One watched Rek leave the next morning. "See you," he called as Rek rose above his head. He turned back into the cave in time to hear Table Scraps.

"Mama, we waited until you came here with Strange One, but now we're going too."

"Going?" she asked.

"Strange One has his own cave. Now that no human owns us, I want to be on my own too," Table Scraps said.

"So do I," said Truffle.

"Me, too," added Seven.

"Besides," explained Nasturtium, "this isn't a good place for pigs. We'll be able to find more food in the lower woods."

Buttercup puffed, "It was really hard to climb here. I still don't feel like I can catch my breath."

"So we go find a cave farther down the mountain. Not a problem," said Gwendolyn.

"But I'm staying here in my cave," Strange One reminded her.

"So the rest of us will all move to a lower cave and come visit you," Gwendolyn proposed. "Still not a problem."

Table Scraps huffed.

"That might not be a good idea, Mama," said Strange One. "I want to find dragons who don't want to live by the leader's rules—dragons like Rek. But other dragons might eat pigs. It won't be safe for you here."

"Then you'll visit the rest of us," Gwendolyn said. "See, still no problem."

Strange One smiled. *I like that—close but I still have a separate place.*

Table Scraps huffed again.

This time the others paid attention. "I didn't mean that I just want to live in a separate place for pigs," he said. "I want to be on my own and have my own adventures."

Strange One looked at the other piglets who nodded in agreement with Table Scraps. *Makes sense to me.*

"Pig," said Duck, "I've told you, all children leave the nest. Isn't it enough that you know Strange One has the soul of a pig, and, with his dragon fire, we saved the piglets?"

Duck understands.

"Yes," said Gwendolyn.

Strange One smiled. *And so does Mama.*

"No." Gwendolyn changed her answer. "It's really not enough!"

Now what?

Duck stretched herself up as tall as possible. "Yes, it is enough. You did your work—you raised your children as best you could. You even did a passable job with an egg. Now your work as a mother is to stop treating them like children. It's not too soon. You've taught all of them what they need to know. Your children are ready."

"But I'm not re . . ."

"Posh," interrupted Duck. "You weren't ready to raise a dragon either, but not only did you teach him everything he needs to know, you raised a dragon who's trustworthy and brave."

"You think I'm trustworthy and brave!"

"Don't let it go to your head, lizard. And I still question your judgement in friends."

"But Rek . . ." *Now isn't the time to argue with Duck.*

"Mama," Strange One said, "If I hadn't left the farm and gone away by myself, the farmer would have given me away. I wouldn't have rescued the piglets."

"This could be my chance to do something fantastic like Strange One did," argued Table Scraps. "Maybe something even better!"

"Better? Like what?" asked Strange One.

"I don't know yet, but something better."

Nasturtium shook her head. "Mama," she said, "remember when you said you weren't sorry you went to the dragon's cave? We want to be brave too and have our own stories."

Table Scraps stamped his hoof. "Besides, I'm not a piglet any more. I don't need anybody's permission to do anything!"

He turned to Strange One. "And I don't need you to protect me from dragons. Mama outsmarted them, and I can too!"

Nasturtium nuzzled Gwendolyn. "We'll love you always, Mama. You gave us everything, even a dragon for a brother. What other pigs can say that? I'll come find you soon."

Nasturtium turned to Strange One. "Bye, big brother. I love you too."

She was the first to leave.

One by one, the other piglets leaned against Gwendolyn for a moment, touched noses with Strange One, and said goodbye to Duck before they followed Nasturtium out of the cave and down the mountain.

Buttercup was last. "I want to see where everyone is going, Mama."

She rushed out and hollered, "Hey, wait for me!"

Gwendolyn seemed frozen. "I don't know what to do if I'm not taking care of my children," she whispered.

Strange One didn't know what to do or say.

"Pig," said Duck, "just go back to doing what made you happy before the piglets were born."

Good idea, Duck.

"Well," said Gwendolyn, "I always liked going to the pond and talking to you."

"Fine," said Duck. "We'll do that again when I come back in the spring."

"In the spring?" Strange One and Gwendolyn echoed.

"I'm not staying for the snows! Think of something else you liked to do."

"I liked when Ruthe talked to me and scratched my ears. But I can't do that either," Gwendolyn groused.

"If all you want to do is talk, chickens make great friends," Duck snipped.

"Since I can't go back to the farm, I can't do that either, even if I wanted to," Gwendolyn snapped back.

They look so angry! This isn't going well. "What else did you do before we were born?" Strange One asked in desperation.

"I explored the farm."

"Well, finally, there you go," quacked Duck. "You can explore the woods on your way down the mountain. Now I need to leave and try to catch up with my flock."

Her voice softened, "You are the most interesting friend I've ever had. I'll find you in the spring, Pig."

She abruptly turned to Strange One. "Don't forget what I taught you about flying." Duck waddled out of the cave.

Gwendolyn and Strange One looked at each other.

Strange One's feelings swirled. *What should I say to her? What's the most important thing?*

"I'm glad you were the one who found my egg," he blurted. "I love you."

"I'm glad you are the one who hatched," she answered. "I love you, too"

With a tight throat and tears in his eyes, Strange One watched Gwendolyn leave.

She could stay and live in one of the tunnels. I'd still have Rek. They like each other. Isn't that enough?

Strange One started to call Gwendolyn back. But his heart spoke a second truth. *No, it's not enough. Maybe there are more dragons who want a different kind of life. I have to find out.*

CHAPTER 41

I can travel through lonely shadows to come to places of light.

Alone and in deep shadows, Gwendolyn stumbled down the mountainside.

Every time life seems perfect, something spoils it. We all reunited when Strange One rescued the piglets. Then the piglets decided to leave.

Before that, the piglets were ready to move to new farms. Then I found out that Ruthe and the farmer planned to sell some for food.

Gwendolyn shivered in the shade. She felt squeezed small by loneliness, as if she no longer belonged anywhere.

Before that, I found an egg. I just wanted to know what would hatch. When it did, I had to worry about a dragon eating the piglets . . .

I was so frightened about what Strange One might do. But without him . . . Gwendolyn trembled. She didn't want to finish her thought.

She pushed a branch aside. *Too bad I admitted I wasn't sorry I went to the dragon's cave. If I hadn't said it, the piglets wouldn't think it was all right to go off into the forest looking for their own adventures.*

What I learned in the dragon's cave saved Strange One's life, helped him get fire, and saved the piglets. Maybe good will come from the piglets leaving too.

Gwendolyn's brain seemed to spiral. She tried to remember

Duck's words—something about looking for happiness in the things that she liked before she had her children.

I liked to sing. She tried to make up a song.

"Life full of pain. Life full of sorrow."

This isn't helping. I'm not ready for my children to not need me. A shaft of sunlight pierced a break in the trees. As Gwendolyn stepped into it, she remembered an older song.

"Sun warming my back,"

The autumn sunshine felt like a blessing. The shaft of light seemed a crack that revealed a glimpse into a bigger world.

The last time I sang that song, I found an egg in a compost pile. I wasn't ready to raise a dragon or travel to the she-dragon's cave. But the struggle and the pain were part of the good.

Duck's right. I did teach my children to take care of themselves. I am a good mother.

She stepped back into shade. *I can travel through lonely shadows to come to places of light.*

Gwendolyn smiled. *My piglets want to be brave like me! Table Scraps thinks Strange One is his competition. I'll just have to show him his mother is still in the running. I can't wait to find out what I'm not ready for this time!*

CHAPTER 42

Where's the edge?

*W*hen *Mama said the words to give me fire, she said "Loving starts with family."* **Starts** *with family. I love my family, and it doesn't end there.*

I was afraid to go to the gathering. But if I hadn't, I wouldn't have met Rek. He wouldn't be my friend.

Strange One walked out of his cave. He gazed at the valley below and then looked up to the sky.

It's all so wide. Where's the edge? Strange One spread his wings as far as possible and stood tall. The image of the rooster flashed in his mind. *The rooster did his best to protect his flock. The dragon leader didn't protect anyone but himself. Maybe there's a whole flock of dragons out there who want to be dragons, but different. Maybe they're brave enough to be strange.*

DISCUSSION QUESTIONS

After chapters 3 and 4:

How important do you think names are? Do you like your name? How did you get it or why did you pick it out for your child?

What do you think a baby feels when it is being born or hatched?

After chapters 5 and 6:

Why do you think the farmer and Duck want to get rid of the dragon? Do you think they have good reasons?

What kinds of things do brothers and sisters argue about?

After chapter 11:

Can you think of one species raising another? What happens? Do you think Gwendolyn will be able to teach Strange One to be a dragon?

What do you think your parents should teach you that they may not know themselves? How do you think they could do that?

What do you think your child may need to know in life that you don't know yourself? How do you think you can prepare your child?

After chapter 14:

What do you treasure? Why?

After chapter 15:

Tell about a time you laughed so hard your stomach hurt.

Does a dragon have to be able to breath fire? Why or why not?

Tell about a time you did something brave.

After chapter 20:

Was there a time you scared somebody else? Tell about it. How did it feel?

Have you ever been praised for something you didn't feel good about?

Tell about something you did to keep yourself safe.

After chapter 23:

How are Gwendolyn and the she-dragon different as mothers? Is there any way they are alike?

After chapter 26:

Why do you think Strange One wants to leave? Why does Gwendolyn want him to stay? Who's right?

After chapter 28:

What does Strange One need? What do you need?

After chapter 30:

If you were Strange One, would you go to the gathering? Why or why not?

Can you make up a riddle for Strange One's name?

After chapter 34:

Tell about a time you felt alone.

If you were Strange One, would you tell Rek he could leave? Why or why not?

After chapter 36:

Do you think Strange One should let Rek come? Why or why not?

After chapter 38:

How do you think Strange One feels about Ruthe and the farmer? Can you feel more than one thing for somebody?

After chapter 42:

What do you think Gwendolyn will do?

What do you think Strange One will do?

Acknowledgments

It takes a village to raise a book. Here are some of the fantastic people I get to thank for helping my dream come true:

The Barracudas, a group of funny, supportive, and tough-as-nails writers, were the midwives for this book. I love you and miss you. You taught me so much.

Later critique groups helped with my book child's growth: the Writeaways and my SCBWI group. I love you too. Thank you all.

Thanks to: Rita Mailheau for proof-reading with an editor's sensibility ritamailheau@gmail.com; Dan Miller for creating the cover, www.4-dan-miller.artistwebsites.com and blog at www.ImpressionEvergreen.com; the editors who rejected this book before it was truly finished; friends and relations who helped with their interest and encouragement.

Deepest gratitude and love to my husband Britt Palmer and son Matt Jones for being who they are. Britt repeatedly reads, listens, pushes, and supports in so many ways including drawing the chapter icons. He's another dream come true. Matt repeatedly criticizes, challenges, and makes me laugh. I'm so grateful he's the kid I got to raise.

And thank you, as they said in the old books, Dear Reader. A book that isn't read is never more than half way complete. Thank you for spending time with *Secrets of the Flame*. I'd love to hear from you and can be reached through my blog at www.hundredbookpileup.com or through my e-mail at piganddragon@cox.net

About the only thing I'm lacking is someone I can blame for my lapses.

ABOUT
THE
AUTHOR

 Cindy Schuricht is a retired elementary school teacher who misses her first graders, but loves having time to write. She and her husband live in Southern California with the youngest of revolving sons and three cats. Cindy's middle-grade fantasy, *The Pig and the Dragon*, is being reissued with the new title, *Secrets of the Flame*. Cindy's blog focuses on recommending children's books to adults, such as parents, teachers, or grandparents, for children or for the child within. You can find it at www.hundredbookpileup.com